MW00622377

FULL
SPEED
TO A
CRASH
LANDING

ALSO BY BETH REVIS

★Coming soon from DAW

FULL SPEED TO A CRASH LANDING

BETH REVIS

DAW BOOKS

NEW YORK

This is a work of fiction. Names, characters, places, and incidents are
products of the author's imagination or are used fictitiously. Any resemblance
to actual events, locales, or persons, living or dead, is entirely coincidental.

Jacket design by Adam Auerbach
Book design by Fine Design
Edited by Navah Wolfe
DAW Book Collectors No. 1965

DAW Books
An imprint of Astra Publishing House
dawbooks.com
DAW Books and its logo are registered trademarks of
Astra Publishing House

Printed in the United States of America

Library of Congress Cataloging-in-Publication Data

Names: Revis, Beth, author.
Title: Full speed to a crash landing / Beth Revis.
Description: First edition. | New York : DAW Books, 2024. |
Series: DAW book collectors ; no. 1965
Identifiers: LCCN 2024014030 (print) | LCCN 2024014031 (ebook) |
ISBN 9780756419462 (hardcover) | ISBN 9780756419479 (e-book)
Subjects: LCGFT: Science fiction. | Romance fiction. | Novellas.
Classification: LCC PS3618.E895 F85 2024 (print) |
LCC PS3618.E895 (ebook) | DDC 813/.6--dc23/eng/20240408
LC record available at https://lccn.loc.gov/2024014030
LC ebook record available at https://lccn.loc.gov/2024014031

First edition: August 2024
10 9 8 7 6 5 4 3 2 1

DEDICATION

This book is dedicated to spite,
my greatest muse and motivator.

EPIGRAPH

Look, I don't have the cash to pay for a quote from Bruce Springsteen, so just put on "Dancing in the Dark" while you read. It's probably better that way, anyway.

1

So.

I'm not in an ideal situation right now.

I've got ten percent of air left in this portable tank. Ship's been decompressed, which . . . not great. Have to rely on the tank. Okay. Okay. I've got maybe an hour of air left.

But I also know for a fact that there's another ship here. It's the competition, sure, but my radar shows they're in range, and surely a fellow scavenge ship wouldn't be so ruthless to ignore a distress call?

"Come on, come on," I mutter, staring at the slowly blinking communication light. I sent out the signal back when I still had half a day of air left. This nearby ship, I can tell on the radar, it's big, so there's got to be a whole operation going on, crew and everything. It's not a little rig like what I have. So, even if I'm the competition to them, I wouldn't be much of one.

Plus, my ship has a hole on one side. A big one.

The air gauge ticks down to nine percent.

The comm light blinks.

Eight.

Blink. Blink.

Seven.

"You have *got* to answer this comm signal!" I scream at it, deeply aware that takes extra air. I'd like to punch something, but gravity's out on the ship too, which means if I hit the console, I'd just fly backward in the opposite direction. Ricocheting around my own ship doesn't seem like a good use of my limited time.

Blink.

Blink.

The other ship is *not* that far away. It's been well within range for the past hour. What are they all doing, just laughing at a distress signal and rubbing their hands with the knowledge that my ship, though damaged, is another one to loot?

They're not going to let me die, right?

. . . *Right?*

Blink.

And then—

"Hello?" It's staticky and dim, but it's an *answer*.

"Hello, yes?" I say. The ship's signal's already routed to my earpiece. "Took you long enough to answer!"

"You're not authorized to be in this sector," a different voice says, one that rings with authority and contempt.

"Neither are you!" I take a deep breath, then silently

curse as the gauge ticks down another percent. "If you're going to get nitpicky about laws, you ignored a live distress signal for hours." I can hear them start to answer, but I plow on. "And now I'm down to six percent in my air tank."

"What?" The first voice again, sounding a little confused. Male, I think. "This is a *real* distress call?"

"It is for the next thirty minutes or so, because after that, it'll just be body removal," I snap. "My ship had a breach. I'm in a suit, breathing what's left of the only tank I've got."

"What are you even doing out here?"

"Can I answer that when I have more than half an hour left to breathe?" I say, eyes wide at the shock of how dim this other crew is.

"We've got a lock on your signal. You really only got half an hour?"

"Mm-hm." I'm too tense to put it into words, but I try to get the full gravity of the situation in that grunt.

"We'll be cutting it close."

Great. *Great.*

"I'll try to hold my breath, then," I say. Because what the fuck else can I say? I can't exactly refill an oxygen tank in a breached ship.

Whoever answered my call sends me a locator signal. My radar picked them up in this sector, but they've got some basic anti-detection shields up, so I didn't have an exact location. They really aren't far, but are they near enough? I check my tank again. I don't like this. I don't like cutting it *this* close.

But I can't risk doing this any other way.

I stare out the hull window. The planet below curves into view. I've been in orbit for about a week. First to the scavenge site. Not an easy haul. When I picked up the other ship approaching, I knew I couldn't compete with them, even if I'd only finished half the job.

A breach in my cargo hold followed by explosive decompression and total life support failure hadn't exactly been in the original plan. But what's a girl to do? I know how to improvise.

The air tank gauge flashes red before my locator shows the larger ship moving closer to me. I'm at two percent by the time they're in sight, and I'm taking shallow sips of air, keeping still, trying my best to convince my body that oxygen's optional.

I was right. Not about oxygen; things are going to get real dicey soon on that front. I was right about the other ship. It's a big one. Maybe even government-issue. It's not a looter, that's for sure; it's far too sleek and new. I bet every part of that ship is original, not held together by cheap welds and luck like my little *Glory*.

Another voice clicks onto my comm. "D-class, our scans show your breach."

"Did you think I was lying?" I mutter.

"Do you have a port for our cofferdam?"

"Yeah, that's part of the problem," I say. The breach broke the airlock system. Again, plans awry, improvisation, the usual.

"How are you going to—"

I do not have time to mince words. "Get as close as you can," I say. I had my foot latched to a hold bar, but I let go and twist around, already heading aft, using the bars to propel myself through the micrograv as I float down the corridor. I go through the bulkhead door, the heavy metal seals wide open to allow me passage. Straight to the ripped-out hole blown in one side of my ship. "If you pull up starboard and open an airlock transfer, I should be able to get to you without a cofferdam."

"Without a . . . D-class, how are going to—"

"I have a name," I say. "Ada Lamarr, nice to meet you, thank you for saving my life." I'm already at the hole in the side of my ship, careful to avoid the sharp edges of metal that could compromise my suit. I stare out at the massive A-class vessel sidling up alongside my little bird. Dozens of positioning thrusters blow out, edging the leviathan a little closer to me. I scan the side of the ship. Various portholes, a few cargo loader arms, a large shuttle bay—there. An escape airlock hatch for emergency use.

"D-class—Lamarr, exactly how do you intend to reach the *Halifax?*"

Halifax. Old name. Classic. Maybe not government-issue.

"I'm at one percent," I mention as if it weren't my life with minutes to spare. "Can you maybe just trust me on this and open up a door?"

I hold my breath—ironically—and count a few more seconds down. Midship, the airlock door on the side of the *Halifax* pops open.

"Thanks," I say. "See you in a bit." I check my suit and fling myself into the void.

An object in motion stays in motion, that's what Newton said, and the proof of it's here in space. As I kick off the side of my ship, past the jagged metal edges of the hole, I would keep going forever through the black at this exact same speed and direction if I didn't hit something. I mean, I'm *hoping* I hit the *Halifax*, which is absolutely my intent, but if that fails, I'll either get sucked into the gravity of the planet below us—unlikely, given my weight compared to the planet—or I'll, you know, float in the empty black void of space until I die.

Which, according to my air gauge, is any second now.

I'm missing my target. The *Halifax* is coming at me a little quicker than I'd thought. Turns out flying through space without a tether can fuck up your concept of relative locations. Also, while it looks pretty certain I'm going to hit the side of this other ship, I'm not at the best angle to hit the open airlock, which is what I need in order to actually *board* the ship.

My O$_2$ tank may be almost empty, but my propulsion tank is aces. I ignite the jetpack, which does speed me up but at least also speeds me up in the right direction. That little door open on the side of the *Halifax* is calling my name, and even when I reverse the thrusters, I still come in hot enough to slam into the interior door. I would've bounced right off it, but I have the wherewithal to grab on to the latch and hold as the outer door seals shut behind me.

I get a blur of faces at the porthole, a flurry of movement behind the interior wall. This is a classic hyperbaric chamber airlock—a tiny room with one door that opens to the outside, one door that opens to the inside. The inside door won't open until the chamber is repressurized and air's pumped back in. Even as the outer door seals shut, I'm still floating. There's no gravity, no pressure, no air.

Which is a damn shame because there's also no oxygen left in my tank. I suck at nothing, my lungs left wanting. I get up to the porthole window, and through the heavy carbonglass and the thick protection of my helmet, it's hard to see too clearly who's on the other side. I bang on the window with a gloved fist, but I know it's pointless. They can't hurry up a hyperbaric chamber. It's a failsafe to prevent someone from getting the bends and gravity sickness with the artificial grav generator, but at this point, I'd trade that for some air. Black dots dance behind my eyes. *Glory's* chamber can take up to five minutes to normalize, but she's an older model. I can probably hold my breath two minutes?

My feet hit the floor, then my knees. Gravity's back on. I can barely think; my body keeps trying to breathe air that's not there. My panicked heartbeat in my ears doesn't distract me from the *emptiness* of my lungs, a sensation I've never had before. Screw decompression sickness—I rip my helmet off. Bent over, my body makes a gagging-gasping noise. The air is too thin. *But there* is *air,* I think, registering that I can actually hear that dying-choking sound streaming out of my raw throat—no sound waves without air.

My arms give out, and I fall fully on the floor, face against the metal. My body bucks, my shoulders spasming as I gasp at air too thin to fully inflate my lungs. My vision goes red.

The last thing I think before it all goes black is:

Fuck.

2

’m so *cold*.

No, wait. It's just my nose that's cold. That's odd. I squint my eyes open a fraction, then immediately regret that choice and also every choice in my life that led up to this moment of lights so blindingly white that they pierce straight into my brain and fry whatever remaining thoughts I might have.

"Ama Lamarr?" a voice asks gently.

"Ada," I correct automatically.

"Wow, she's alive." A different voice, one a little farther away, mildly surprised.

"I'm not too certain of that," I grumble. I lift an arm, but that arm feels like a million pounds, so I drop it again. My mouth feels weird. I flop my tongue out—too dry—and try to figure out why everything feels cold again.

Hands grab for me and pull me to a sitting position, a croaking groan escaping my lips. I risk opening my eyes again. It still hurts, but it's better than being in the dark.

I'm on a floor, legs splayed, and a small bald woman with dark skin is crouching in front of me, eyes concerned. She

nudges my shoulder gently, and I realize there's a wall behind me. I lean against it, slumping immediately. That takes
a lot out of me, so I suck in some air, and that's when I realize where the weird cold is coming from—a nasal tube is
blowing pure oxygen into me.

"Here," the woman tells me, thrusting a bottle into my
hands. I chug it, and icy liquid slithers down my throat. I'm
so tired of cold. I'm so tired in general.

"My name is Nandina Mohammed," the woman says.
She's the gentle voice. I like her a lot.

"Nice to meet you," I croak. "I think my eyes have hemorrhaged."

She nods. "That was a close call."

I gulp some more water. "Don't get me wrong, super
grateful to not be dead," I say, "but what the fuck took so
long?" I tip my head back, thunking it against the metal
wall, and peer up at the other people. While Nandina is
now on her knees, scanning me with something white and
flashy and important-looking, there are three other people
standing nearby, scowling as if they're deeply perturbed by
the inconvenience of my rescue.

"Hello," I say, waving cheerily at them with my left
hand as Nandina scans my right arm.

"Pulse elevated," Nandina mutters.

"It's been an exciting evening." I think I see her bite

back a smile. I glance up at the other people still staring down at me. No reaction. Tough crowd.

The short white woman in front stands with her legs apart, arms crossed, taking up as much room as her petite frame is capable of. Unconsciously, I think. She wears a tight-fitting jacket that has a line of red at the collar. Noted. This ship is large but not large enough for the captain to literally wear a badge of her rank, just the color stripe. She's got a hard face. Looks like a planner, and I didn't file the triplicate form to be added to the agenda.

The person just behind her and a little to the left has broad shoulders and big muscles. Seems a little jumpy, eyes darting around, looking for danger in this well-lit corridor tastefully tiled in white enamel and accented with chromium. On the captain's other side is a man with unkempt hair. Average size, average build. Totally forgettable. Except for the sharpest, clearest hazel eyes I've ever seen. I shudder. From the cold air, obviously. Then Nandina rips off the nasal tube, and I flinch at the sudden movement.

"You're back up to normal levels," she says.

"That's me," I say. "Normal." I've got my eyes on the trio looming over us. The captain ignores the big person— despite the military bearing, they seem to be a subordinate. She keeps turning to the other man, and I'm starting to think maybe the captain's not as in charge as she wants to be.

"Well, not quite normal." Nandina's a smiler. She looks to the captain. "I'd like to get her to the med bay."

"I'd like to get her off my ship," the captain says.

"Got any mechanics who can fix *my* ship's life support and also the three-meter hole in the side?" I ask.

Her eyes flick to the airlock. Just a quick movement, nothing more, but the meaning is clear. She doesn't need to fix my ship to toss me back outside. It's an idle threat.

Probably.

"This is going to be a fun stay aboard Hotel *Halifax*." I attempt a grin, but it costs too much energy to sustain for more than a second.

"This is a working mission that cannot afford to be interrupted by—" the burly person starts, and then the captain interrupts them.

"First, take our 'guest' to the med bay for Mohammed."

I push against the wall, trying to get my legs to work enough to get me into a standing position, but my feet slip. When I got into the *Halifax*'s hyperbaric chamber, I was wearing a full suit. Now my boots are gone. I took my helmet off myself already, before I passed out. Panic flares inside me. I *need* my suit. *My* suit. I whip my head around as the first officer steps closer to me, the effect making me dizzy. Bile rises up in my throat, but I swallow it down, frantically trying to see through the red haze.

Light fingers tap my hand. My head sloshes forward,

looking down at Nandina's touch, then back up into her concerned face.

"My boots," I gasp.

"Right over there," Nandina says, pointing. My helmet's beside them, and so is my LifePack. Shit, I was panicking about boots, and they're nothing compared to the backpack-like device I have to attach to my suit that holds everything I need to not die out in the black. Air, the jetpack, temp and pressure units. Worth more than the boots. And I've upgraded that shit, personalized the rig to hit my every need.

"First," the captain says impatiently. I assumed the person was the first officer, but I wonder if it's actually their name? Perhaps they prefer the title to a name. Either way, First scoops me up, arms under my knees and around my shoulders, like I'm a fussy baby.

"Hey!" I say.

Nandina stands too, as if this is all perfectly routine. She starts down the corridor, First following behind, stoically looking forward to pretend I'm not flopping around in their arms. "I'm coming back for my stuff!" I say as loudly as my ragged voice can allow. "Do *not* steal my stuff!"

The captain's eyes widen just a little, which, frankly, is rude. That's a good suit. It saved my life. I mean, it also almost killed me when it ran out of air, but *before* that, it saved my life. Plus, the jetpack cost extra. It's really fancy, if I do say so myself.

Behind her, the man who doesn't seem to miss a thing pushes forward and follows First. I rest my head on First's shoulder and blink up at the man trailing behind us. He's dressed in a brown shirt, simple but neat. My eyes slowly glide up and down him, and they find nothing at all objectionable. He's *so* average—height, weight, everything—but there's something about him that tells me he's the most interesting person aboard this ship. After me, obviously. I don't know why I keep looking at him. Tan skin, brown hair cut neatly. If I had to pick a word to describe him, it'd be *trim*. But he's got this air about him, like he knows how the whole universe fits together, and that makes me wonder how I might fit into his carefully organized world. Does he have a slot for chaos, or am I going to have break some stuff to make room on the shelf for me? Either route poses fun and exciting possibilities.

"Hello," I tell the man trailing behind us. I try to sound casual, like this is a routine day, being cradled by a big hulking person on my way to a med bay while I have hemorrhaged eyes and a mouth that had all the saliva boiled out of it, but my voice is still all scratchy and raw and my ears are slightly ringing, so I'm not even sure if I got both syllables out.

The man smiles. "Hello," he says back. Oh, good. He's going to pretend this is normal too. I immediately like him even more.

"You know," I say, wiggling so I don't have to crane my neck around quite so much, "if you'd waited, I bet First would have carried you to the med bay, too."

First grunts.

"I don't mind walking," the man says.

"But consider this: you could be *not* walking. And carried. Like a baby."

"It does look comfortable."

First turns a corner, and glass doors slide open. I'm trying to think of something quippy and witty and charming to say about how comfortable First's arms are, but then they dump me on a table that's lacking in the padding department, and my breath comes out with a little *oof*.

After dropping me, First heads back out the door. The man who followed us here looks around, unsure of where to stand, but eventually leans against the wall, watching us. Nandina is already at the table by the bed, various scanners beeping and, presumably, scanning.

"You're recovering just fine," Nandina says. She holds up a small bottle. "You want to do the eye drops, or would you like me to?"

"Ugh," I say, but I take the bottle.

"Three drops, each eye."

I lean back and put the medicine in my eyes. It feels slimy for an instant, but the more I blink, the better my vision seems. Less red, anyway.

My suit is already partially exposed, the seal-tight released and the inner zipper showing the top portion of my chest.

"This is a good suit," Nandina says.

"Thanks. It was ridiculously expensive—"

"Now strip."

I blink at her. "Not even dinner first?"

She chuckles. "You've got some mild muscle tears. And a little atrophy. How long have you been in space this round? You really need to have some proper gravity every three turns."

"Medics always say that." It wasn't hard to guess what Nandina's role on the *Halifax* is, but I appreciate the twinkle in her eye at the acknowledgment.

"I'm guessing you've not seen solid ground for at least six turns." Nandina gives me a stern look, hands on her hips.

Beyond her I catch a glimpse of the good-looking man, gaze as razored as ever. "Seven," I say, watching him even as I answer her. It's like I can see tiny gears inside his brain, winding around everything I say. "Or eight? Maybe five. Who can remember, really?" I wait until he focuses on me and shoot him a grin.

Oh, a poker face. Nice. Totally gonna break that.

"You take your vits, right?" Nandina says. "Also, I wasn't joking."

"About what?"

"Strip."

She's the doc, but a quick glance at Eyes tells me he has

no intention of leaving, and there's not a curtain for privacy in this med bay. It's all bright white lights and exposed beds.

"Dinner after," Nandina promises.

I have to lean back to get the next part of the seal-tight open. "If you're getting a sneak peek, at least let me know your name," I say, my tone light. I shrug out of the shoulders of my suit and meet the man's eyes.

"Rian White," he says in a voice that counteracts all that cold that had been coursing through me.

Some men have the attitude that there are no bras in space. Which is bullshit. But while Sharp-Eyes Rian White may keep a stony blank face, there's a nice little flush when I don't break eye contact with him as I push my suit down to my hips.

"Good enough," Nandina says. She slaps a few med patches on my mostly bare back, which stings for a second, but there's some excellent stuff in those things. My body gets all good and woobly. Nandina helps me get rid of the rest of the insulated thermal radiation suit. I have the thin version, which is nice, but it's still clunky, and we have to take our time, not risking a tear. I could do it all by myself, but it'd be rough in my current condition. And slow. There are times when stripping slowly is preferable, but now's not it.

First walks back in, sees me half-undressed, and immediately looks up at the ceiling. They've brought my Life-Pack, helmet, and boots, and they hold both laden arms out until Nandina relieves them of the burden, stowing them in a storage locker. The medic hands me some standard-issue— a tunic-style shirt that hangs loosely on me and drawstring pants. Rubber-soled slide-ons are the final touch. It's all a lot more comfortable than my suit and boots, but comfort doesn't matter. After folding my suit up and stowing it with the boots and helmet, Nandina starts to hook up the intakes and chargers on my LifePack, starting with the O_2 tank.

Nandina pauses after that, the fuel charger in one hand. She glances back at me, a question on her lips that I answer before she can ask. "That's a jaxon jet," I say, smug in the knowledge that everyone in the room will be suitably impressed. I take a quick glance around. Maybe they didn't hear me. "A *jaxon* jetpack."

"Oh," Nandina says, but it's clear she doesn't understand the depth of importance that type of jetpack entails. Jaxon fuel, found on the terran worlds in at least two colonial systems, is extremely difficult to mine, but the best of the best. Most suits have basic units, but a jaxon-fueled jetpack burns cold and lasts forever. It's stable, efficient, and reliable, with precise positioning controls. Other jets can get you up in the air; a jaxon lets you soar like a dragon.

Nandina looks at the charger unit in her hand, the one that doesn't have anywhere to go. "So, does that mean I don't have to hook it up—"

"Yeah." I glance at the others. "It's fine; you can leave

it." No one here appreciates good tech. Nandina closes the locker door after connecting the other elements of my Life-Pack to the recharger.

First is still staring at the ceiling, waiting for me to give them the all clear that I'm dressed. "Are you going to carry me to dinner?" I ask. "Because that would be nice."

"You can walk now." Nandina's reading those scanners again.

"Just because I can doesn't mean I should." My words are slurring a little. I bat my eyes at Rian. "Or you can carry me."

"I didn't take you for a damsel in distress," he comments. Nandina puts some more patches on me—two just under my clavicle—and I start to feel a little more sober. Caffeine patches, I think, or maybe some adrenaline to counteract the relaxers. Up and down, up and down.

"Damsel, yes," I say. "Distress? Never."

"Not even when you're running out of air?"

I flash him my best grin. "Not even then."

3

Nandina wasn't lying. Dinner waits for me in the mess hall. Real food, too, an *actual* meal.

It comes with an audience. The captain's there, and First takes up a position right beside her, at least until she tells them to go back to the bridge and "monitor." Which means, of course, there's something—or someone—to monitor. I tuck into the tray in front of me—there's protein goop in the slop, but the bumpy bits have to be actual, real lentils, which is nice, and whether the leaves spotting the mix are rehydrated or not, I absolutely appreciate the chance to eat something green that's not a by-product of recycler worms.

The captain talks to Nandina, who, after assuring her I'm healthy, not carrying some weird alien plague, and unlikely to die anytime soon, is sent away. I wave at her, and she waves back. Such a nice doctor.

Rian White stays. He sits down across from me even when the captain remains standing. And the captain doesn't like that. And he doesn't care. And these lentils are really good.

"Are there seconds?" I ask.

Rian looks like he's going to offer more, but the captain snaps, "No."

I lick my spoon. "Any hot sauce?"

"No," she says again.

"Ah, you guys get real food on the regular, then. If you were using worms, you'd have a whole tank of hot sauce."

Rian cringes, the look of a guy who knows how little hot sauce does for the aftertaste but how important it is anyway.

"What are you doing in this sector?" the captain asks.

"You can sit, you know," I say, gesturing with the spoon. "It's a little awkward just staring up at you like this." I said that to be nice, because she's short enough to not hear that kind of thing often, but she just keeps scowling. "I don't even know your name."

"I'm the captain of the *Halifax*," the captain of the *Halifax* says.

"Yes, but Captain *what?*" I ask. Her jaw tightens. Oh, this one does *not* like being questioned. Not even for a name. I wonder if she's had interrogation training. I wonder if she's *just* had interrogation training for this mission.

"Ursula, just sit," Rian says.

I shoot him a grin. "Yes, please do, Ursula."

"Captain Io," she snaps. But she does at least sit.

"So, I'm guessing I'm here for the same reason you're

here," I say cheerily, scraping the spoon along the bottom of the tray. "Salvage. The UGS *Roundabout* is not going to loot itself, after all."

"You are not supposed to know about the UGS *Round-about*," Ursula says.

I give her an exaggerated wink. "And neither are you."

"How did you get here so quickly?"

I pick up the metal tray and lick the bottom. When I put it down, Ursula and Rian are both waiting for my answer.

"I didn't get here any quicker than my ship can go." I shrug. "Then again, I think I blew a fuel line, so maybe I ran a *little* hot."

"Ms. Lamarr," Rian starts.

"Mr. White." I match his deep tone.

"How long have you been at this site?"

I shrug. "Two standard days."

"The UGS *Roundabout* only crashed ten cycles ago. This is not a typical route. From almost any port, you'd have to have come here within hours of the crash to be here before us."

"Look, you know I'm not going to tell you my source," I say, leveling with him. "Looters' code."

"Looters don't have a code," Ursula protests, a distinct snarl to her voice.

"Are you saying you don't have a code? No wonder you almost let me die before deigning to rescue me." There's an edge in my voice now. "Because, see, the law says a ship

crash can be scavenged if it's not reported by the government as off-limits. And *Roundabout*'s not been reported. So,
I'm in the right here, and just because you don't like that
don't mean I'm breaking the law."

My gaze slides from the captain over to Rian. "But *you*,
on the other hand, ignored a distress call for *hours*."

And that *is* against the law. Any ship within range of a
distress call must answer the distress call if they have the
means. And clearly, *Halifax* has the means.

The captain squares her shoulders, her eyes narrowed,
but I glare right back at her. She has the grace to shrink a
little. "There was some . . ." She swallows. "Some debate
about the validity of your call."

I raise both my eyebrows. I'm not seeing everything in a
red haze anymore, but I caught a glimpse of myself in a mir-
ror in the med bay, and I know my eyes are still crimson
from the burst blood vessels.

"You have to understand how unlikely it was that you
were here," the captain continues. She doesn't like being in
the wrong, and she's the type of person who wants to talk
her way into being right. She's had too many people believe
her just for speaking, and it shows. "It seemed clear that a
distress signal from this location, at this time, would be sabotage, and . . ."

"And yet it wasn't," I say simply.

Her mouth closes.

"Do you know what it's like to count each breath?" I continue. "Do you know how it feels to pick up a ship's signal, to *know* it's in range, and to be ignored, all while your last oxygen tank gets lower?" I huff a bitter laugh. "I've always known the risks out here. You think I haven't considered them when I'm a single person on an old ship? Something goes wrong out here . . . I know how that ends. I just . . ." I shake my head, the tip of my tongue on my teeth. "I expect to die alone if something goes wrong in the black. I just never thought I'd have an audience who watched without even answering my distress call."

I've made Ursula realize the full depths of how wrong she was. I'm not sure what Rian's role on the *Halifax* is, but no one has higher authority on any ship than the captain. It was her call.

And she made it wrong.

And we all know it. Without question. Even her.

"Ms. Lamarr, I cannot express how sorry I am—" she starts.

"And you won't even give me seconds."

The captain blinks at me, stunned, and there's little nervous tic near her left eye as she stands up, grabs my food tray, and goes over to the dispenser to get me another round of those lentils. "And some leaves!" I call to her.

"It's spinach," she says.

I shrug. A leaf is a leaf, but green stuff? Damn, that's expensive. "Double spinach, please!"

Rian smirks at me. "You're good," he says while Ursula busies herself with the dispenser.

"I am." I grin at him. "At what?"

He doesn't answer. Those eyes of his. They don't miss a thing. I shovel a spoonful of lentils into my mouth as soon as the captain drops the tray in front of me.

"How did you know that the *Roundabout* wrecked?" Rian asks. He doesn't seem impatient that I have to chew; he speaks like this is idle conversation.

"Looter to looter?" I motion him closer, as if I'm going to whisper a secret, then shake my head. "I'm not telling."

"We're not looters." The captain's voice brooks no argument. "We're here to salvage—"

I shrug. "*Salvage* is just a few letters away from *scavenge*. I bet they have the same roots. Probably French. Wild that a country that doesn't even exist anymore can fuck up our language so much."

Rian frowns, and a cute little wrinkle forms on his brow. "I don't think you're right about that."

"We are not here to argue etymology." The captain's voice rises a notch. She can't stand this. She's so to-the-point about everything. She may be short, but even I didn't realize it was going to be this easy to take her measure.

I cut her a little slack. "*Roundabout* wasn't reported. That means it's up for grabs."

"Yes," Rian allows. "But not by you." When he sees my

expression, he grins. "Perhaps if your ship hadn't been breached, maybe you'd be our competition."

"Maybe?!" I gasp, clutching my chest with one hand and scooping up more goop with the other.

"But as it stands, you're just our guest, and that means you can't . . ." He struggles to find the right word.

"Loot," the captain supplies. "You can't loot."

"You can hire me," I say. "I work for cheap. Just feed me and cut me some profits."

"No," Ursula says flatly.

"I got nothing better to do," I assure her. "Plus, I am *very* good at my job."

"No," the captain says again. She stands, turning to Rian and ignoring me completely. "I'll grant her refuge but nothing else."

Oh, good. Despite delaying my rescue, she is the law-abiding sort. Not like there are many witnesses out here; she could toss me from the airlock. But I don't think she's seriously contemplated that option, which is refreshing. Then again, if the *Halifax* is a government-funded ship, which I highly suspect, there's probably already logs of their detour and a registry online that I'm here. Killing me would mean paperwork. I swear, I've been saved at least four times in my life thanks to people who just didn't want to file the damn paperwork on me.

But don't get me wrong. I *am* appreciative of the captain and all her legalese. I automatically like anyone not actively trying to kill me, even if they won't let me have some fun planetside.

"Refuge includes three square meals a day, right?" I ask.

Ursula grunts, which I take for a yes, and then she leaves, ignoring my very polite and friendly farewell.

Rian's watching me. Man, those eyes. "I looked up your ship registry."

I lick my spoon, making a little bit of a show of it, but he pretends not to notice. Cute.

"Surprised that clunker of yours has lasted as long as it did," he adds.

"I can fix her, no worries," I say.

"There's a three-meter-wide hole in the side."

"We all have our flaws."

Rian snorts, clearly not sharing my optimism about *Glory*. "How long have you *really* been at this site?" he asks.

I hesitate.

"I could board your ship and examine the logs," he says.

"By all means." I make a grand gesture. With the coffer-dam link broken, Rian would have to do the same thing I did—jump out of the airlock with a positional suit and board through the breach. Of course, he'd have a full air tank, so maybe it's not as big a deal to him.

"I would rather you just tell me."

"You're going to be trouble for me," I say, sighing romantically.

"Because I ask questions?"

"Because you ask questions with a voice like that."

"Like what?" He looks genuinely confused.

"*I would rather you just tell me.*" I try to emulate his deep voice, smooth as chocolate. Damn, when was the last time I had chocolate?

"I do not sound like that," he deadpans.

"I know, you sound much sexier, but I'm *trying*."

"I don't sound sexy!"

I just raise my eyebrow. Unlike before, I forget for a second that my eyes are stained red and the purple bags under them probably make me look half-dead. Then I remember and grab my spoon, stuffing more lentils into my mouth before I say something else that's dumb.

"Anyway," I say, "you can check the logs if you want, but I only beat the *Halifax* here by two days." Like I already said once, and I don't for a second doubt he knows that. He's testing me, my story. But I'm not going to trip up that easy.

"Did you go down to the crash site?" he asks, all gravity. Nothing hotter than a focused man.

"Yup," I say.

That gets a reaction. I think he expected me to lie or play around.

"What did you find?" he asks.

I shrug. "Metal. As one would expect."

He's silent for so long that I start eating again. I can guess what he's thinking, though.

The *Roundabout* is a cargo ship. One of those big long-haulers. And it *was* taking a path that was out of the way, bypassing the major routes. It was a ship that didn't want to be found.

But it also didn't want to crash, and it did, so clearly, ships don't always get what they want.

"A lot of cargo crates labeled with Fetor Tech stamps," I add. "Is that what you're looking for, tech? I don't bother with that. I don't have the right connections."

Rian doesn't answer.

I put my spoon down. "I don't know what you guys are trying to 'salvage,'" I say, meeting his sharp eyes. "But me? I'm a metal scavenger. And I'm good at it. And that ship wasn't reported, so it's free game."

That's a sticking point for him. If the *Roundabout* had something really, really important on it, then the government would have reported it off-limits. And few people would risk looting it. But that ship had been on a secret path for a reason, I'm betting. And that reason means the government sent over the *Halifax* rather than risk the wrong people noting it was gone.

"It's only been crashed ten cycles," Rian says softly.

There's something different about his eyes now, something sad. "The planet it crashed into isn't exactly hospitable, but . . ."

"You're telling me," I snort. This planet is one of the unnamed ones. Any planet that humans can't settle doesn't get a fancy name, just an alphanumerical designation. And this planet? Definitely can't be settled.

"Ten cycles isn't long enough for . . ." He pauses again, and I finally get his point. "There were thirteen crew members aboard when it crashed."

I look down at my empty tray. "I know," I whisper. "Or I guessed. Ship that size. Had to have human crew. I stayed in the back end."

I can tell he doesn't know what I mean. I prop my elbows on the table and bump my fists together. "Ship like *Roundabout,* it wasn't ever meant to land on a planet. Too big." It's a freighter, so it was built in space. Tenders brought the crew up from the planet to the ship, and it took and offloaded cargo with transport shuttles. "I don't know what went wrong, but she got caught in that planet's gravity. It ripped her in at least two pieces." I pull my fists apart, letting them fall to the table with *thunk*s that make Rian jump. He looks down at my hands, symbolizing that there are two broken parts of the ship, separated by a decent distance.

"Our initial scans showed something like that," he says, almost to himself.

"Your scans were right. Anyway, I stayed aft. Didn't see any bodies. Wasn't looking for them, though."

Rian nods gravely. Crash like that, there wouldn't be survivors. Just corpses.

"I did all my salvaging from the cargo hold," I add.

"What did you take?"

"Metal," I say, shaking my head. We already went over that.

"You didn't look at the cargo?"

"I didn't get a chance. It's . . ." I cringe. "It's a mess down there. Metal's easy. I filled up my haul with the bits on the ground, didn't even need my hover for it."

Rian nods, thinking. But I'm not sure what angle's caught his attention. And that? That's what has *my* attention.

4

First comes back, on the captain's orders, no doubt, and escorts me to a bunk room. The crew's quarters are pretty big. There's space enough here for a crew three or four times the size that the *Halifax* is now hosting. Money doesn't seem to be the problem. Which means they're operating with a tight crew on purpose.

The fewer people you have on board, the less talk you have off.

"Nice digs." I step into the room First offers me. The door slides shut, leaving me alone in the room. "So polite," I mutter to the air.

The room is small but bigger than my bunk on *Glory*. A double-sized bed bolted to the floor dominates one side. The wall by the door hosts a suit rack, complete with re-charger hookups. That's not unusual for a ship like this; crew tend to like to keep their own suits close, and it's easier to dress in one's room and then go to the shuttle bay than to turn the shuttle bay into an impromptu dressing room prior to departure. Of course, this means Nandina didn't have to store my suit in a locker. Which means someone's going to scan it. I file that bit away as I prowl the rest of the room. Wall cubbies show a few more outfits in the same tunic-and-drawstring style—generic gear made available for crew between suited walks, standard issue. The wash unit has some extra gadgets beyond just an antiseptic sponge and a suction toilet, so that definitely meets my approval.

There's a large porthole of carbonglass built along the far wall, and even from here, I can see the curve of the planet below. When I press my face against the window, I can almost catch the empty shell of *Glory* floating nearby, too. My good little ship. "Don't worry," I tell her. "I'm coming back for you."

My eyes linger at the gaping black scar of the breach.

I force myself to turn to the planet. *Protoplanet*, I mean. The world is riddled with earthquakes and volcanos, lava spurts forming dangerously erratic eruptions. It's going to be a nice, big world one day. But right now, that planet is still a baby throwing tantrums about its own tectonic plates.

The porthole is set into the wall, the lip of it forming a space that's perfect for sitting. I lean my back against the curved metal and stretch out my legs. My eyes drift from my poor, broken ship to the poor, broken planet and back again.

I wake up with a start. Who knew lentils were soporific?

The comm by the door beeps again, and I hear Rian's voice. "Ms. Lamarr?"

I hop off the ledge and cross the room. The door slides open at my touch, and there he is, eyes and all.

"Visiting a lady in her bedchamber, my goodness," I say, propping a hip against the door frame.

"I sent off for some more data on your ship," he says. "Can I come in? Or we can discuss this elsewhere."

I step aside. There really isn't much furniture in the room, so I perch back up on the porthole ledge, letting Rian take the bed.

Internally, my mind is calculating what he had to do to get even rudimentary data this quickly. The *Halifax* is obviously on the portal communication system, but even then, he had to have pulled some strings and must be using a booster. Technically, nothing travels faster than light, not even information. The portals just give us shortcuts.

"Tell me all about *Glory*," I say, grinning at him.

Rian juts his chin out, looking down at me. "That's just it. There's hardly any record."

My best grin is smeared all over my face. "Hardly any? That means you found something." Which, shit. I thought I had everything scrubbed.

Rian pulls out a data pad and reads the screen. "Licensed as a salvage; last recorded location was four turns ago. On the other side of the galaxy."

He doesn't say *who* it was licensed to. Nice.

"I'm a busy girl," I say. "I bounce all around."

He watches me, waiting for me to say something else.

"When are you guys going to tell me the super secret thing you're looking for in the *Roundabout* wreckage?" I ask eagerly.

Rian drops the data pad on the bed. "Who says we're looking for anything super secret?" But he's got a wry grin on his face; he expected me to guess this much.

"If you told me and if you sent me down there, I could find it," I tell him. "Save you loads of time."

"We already have a crew planetside."

That explains the empty rooms on this corridor, then. "How many?"

"Two."

Okay, not all the rooms. Still a top-secret project.

I clap my hands together. "Come on; tell me what you're looking for. Precious gems? Hidden treasure? Top-secret government files?"

"My lips are sealed." Rian presses his mouth closed as if to prove the point, although he can't hide the tilting curve of his smile.

"How big is it, at least?" I ask. "No, don't tell me. It's

gotta be small. All the big stuff was in the cargo hold, and you didn't care that I've already been there."

"Didn't I?"

I shake my head at him. "Nah, I can read you like a data scan. Whatever you're looking for, it's gotta be small."

"And you want me to send you down to help search for it?"

"Hey, I'm just trying to be nice. If you and Ursula—"

"Captain Io."

"—want me to just nap and eat for the rest of your mission, whatever it is, I am absolutely, one hundred percent fine with that. I'm a good scavenger, but I'll be honest, where I really excel at life is in eating and napping."

That much is true.

"What are the conditions like down there?" Rian gets off the bed and leans over me, peering through the porthole. The scent of him fills my senses—I can't even describe it; it's just a *clean* smell but something unique to him, something that fills me up.

"It's hot," I say.

My head's leaned back on the porthole, looking up at him, the planet in the corner of my vision. "So hot down there that the suit almost isn't enough. There's a layer of rocky earth, but that planet's new. Stomp too hard and magma comes up."

"That'll make loaders difficult."

"That's not your problem," I say.

"Oh?" He's got one elbow on the carbonglass, and he drops his gaze to me. I'm caged in by his body and the ship, and usually that sort of positioning makes me claustrophobic, but right now, all I really want to do is close the space between us. Instead, I loll my head on the carbonglass, the smooth surface cooling my flushed cheeks.

"You gotta think," I say, looking out at the black, "*Roundabout* crashed *into* the planet. Not *onto* it."

It takes him a second. "So, parts of the ship were engulfed by lava?"

"I'm guessing. I only saw the aft. I'm thinking the full brunt of the impact was forward. The nose of the ship, hitting a barely cooled surface. It's not just the impact you got to worry about; it's also the conditions of the planet fucking everything else up. So, if you're looking for something on the bridge of that ship? It's probably not just crushed but also burned up by lava."

There's a distant look on Rian's face. I'm still facing the window, but I can see his reflection. And he doesn't know that I see the subtle shake of his head, the firm belief that whatever he's looking for is still down there. That's not hope—there's no desperation to his movement. No, he's certain. Whatever he's looking for, it's still there.

He just has to find it.

It's either not on the bridge, or it's protected somehow, I think. And, it goes without saying, it's worth something. A lot of something.

"It makes me wonder what went wrong," Rian says.

He's still focused on the ship. And it's a fair question. All of space, the empty black void, where a ship could just break down and call for help . . . and it crashed. Into a planet. Made of lava.

"It does make salvage difficult," I say. "I'm a lot more used to ghost ships in the black."

Rian glances down at me, but I'm still pretending to look out of the window. "That sounds lonely."

I close my eyes. "It can be."

"Is it always just you and your ship?"

I debate whether or not to tell him the truth. "No," I say finally.

He doesn't ask more, but it's weighing on my mind now. "When it is just me, though, I tend to only do the push jobs." *Glory* can be used as a tugboat, pushing a dead ship through the void of space to a scrapyard station. Size doesn't matter, not in space, not where gravity and friction don't exist.

"This isn't that," Rian points out.

"Nope."

"What made you pick up a dangerous mission like

Roundabout? It's a lot more labor-intensive than just hauling scrap."

I creak open an eyelid. He's watching me. I could feel it even before I looked. And even when I open both my eyes, he doesn't look away.

"Girl's gotta eat," I say, shrugging.

He doesn't buy it, but he lets it slide. That's how I know he knows I'm dancing with lies and half-truths. Someone trying to figure out the truth knows when to let silence do the interrogation. And he thinks he's pegged me and time will make me trust him. He's got sharp eyes, but it's in the way his shoulders are relaxed—he's certain of himself. He's one of those calm guys who just know it won't take anything but time and persistence to get what he wants. He's in a marathon and thinks I'm sprinting.

I kick my legs up on the ledge and turn to the window, really looking down at the planet now. "You wanna know what gets me?" I say.

He makes a curious sound. I can still feel him watching me.

"There's no way you and I both will clear out the wreckage of the *Roundabout*," I say. "Impossible. A matter of mass; there's too much of that broken ship down there for us."

"Other scavengers may eventually come."

"Maybe. But what's the point in hauling up every scrap?

Nah, there's a good chance some of that ship is going to stay on that planet."

"Probably."

"And look at it. I'm not a geologist, but that planet out there? It's a baby. The volcanos and thin crust and the earthquakes . . . it's a planet that's still growing, not yet fully formed. Give it a few million years, and the tectonic plates will settle. Gravity will pull in an atmosphere. Little algae and stuff will grow, then proper plants. Maybe dinosaurs. Another few million, and this planet could host sapient life. We're looking at the beginning of a whole world."

Rian's gaze shifts to the window.

"And there's carbonglass down there," I continue. "Alloy metals that last. I don't know how this stuff works, but the right conditions . . . what if the ship just gets buried and preserved? And in millions and millions of years, whatever life this planet fosters includes archaeologists. And they dig down in just the right spot and they find the *Roundabout*."

"I suppose it's possible, if unlikely."

That's basically the mantra of my life, but I don't bother telling him that. Instead, I say, "That's what I think about. Space is so mind-bogglingly big. Utterly incomprehensible. But we leave our shit everywhere. Ghost ships in the void. Crashes on protoplanets. The litter we jettison. And sometimes, I run into it. It's always our stuff. Never anything from another species."

"There are other species, though," Rian says.

"Yeah, but not sapient." We've found whole planets with life, flora and fauna. Nothing ever talks back to us.

Nothing ever builds spaceships.

"Maybe that planet down there doesn't even develop life," Rian says. "Most of them don't."

That's true. But maybe it will. And maybe there will be someone like me, millions and millions of years from now, who finds something from us, who will know that even if the universe is silent, it wasn't always.

5

I gotta be careful. Rian? He's a distraction. So much so that I almost wonder if that was his intent. He didn't really ask any of the questions I thought he would; he didn't even come close. After he leaves, I go over everything he said, everything I said, and the dots don't connect.

There's an angle here, but I can't see it yet.

So, I go to the med bay.

Nandina's not there when I arrive, but judging from how quickly she pops up, she was close. Or they got some cams watching me when I leave the room. Either's a possibility.

"Are you feeling ill?" she asks.

"Just came for my stuff."

Her eyes widen slightly.

"My suit," I clarify.

"You want your suit?"

"Yes. I'll keep it in my room." It's been enough time on the chargers that the tanks should be full again, but even if they aren't there are recharger ports in the bunk room.

"I can leave it in the locker; it's not a problem."

"I'd rather have it with me." I purposefully bought a suit that was more mobile than some of the ship-specific suits. Between the thincraft material and the jaxon jets, my suit's worth almost as much as my ship. Not that I think anyone on the *Halifax* would pilfer parts.

I just would rather have it with me.

"Of course you can have it," Nandina says, opening up the med bay door and heading to the storage locker. "But . . ."

Why. The question she won't ask. Why am I trying to get a spacesuit in my bunk room.

I wait until she looks at me, and I meet her eyes. "It's the only thing I own on this ship. It's the only thing that's mine."

Nandina's face is an open book, sympathy evident all over her features. She nods and passes the suit over to me. It's awkward in my arms, but it is a comfort to have it. I know I can't just jump out the porthole window of my bunk room, but at least if this ship is breached like *Glory* was, I'll have my suit handy.

"I know it's a little silly," I mutter, hefting my LifePack on my shoulders like a backpack.

"No, I get it." Nandina's trying hard not to show her emotion, but it's futile. She can't help but wear her feelings out in the open. That's what good people do. "But just so you know, if you need anything, anything at all . . . I can help you get it. We have lots of supplies on this ship."

"Thanks." I offer her a watery smile and turn to go. "Actually . . . do you have any data recorders I could have?"

Like I said, an open book. Her surprise is as clear as carbonglass.

"I just thought it may be nice to record some of my thoughts. You know . . . process it all," I explain.

"Oh, of course!" Nandina reaches for a different storage cabinet. "Absolutely; I should have thought of that myself. I get so used to physical medicine, but emotional therapy is just as important. The *Halifax* is a job for me, but your ship was your home, wasn't it?"

I nod, watching as she punches in a key code on the storage locker. Five digits, the last two are zero. On the table beside the locker, there's a scanner.

"I cannot imagine what that loss is like. Journaling is a great idea, but I want you to know that I'm happy to talk as well. Like I said, both the body and the mind are important for full healing, and I'm here to help."

She reaches inside and pulls out a data recorder. It's a little thing, only about the size of my finger, but it's capable of storing a lot of information. Audio, video, text. I check the side. It's got an input port, too—if I had the clearance code, I could download every single bit of data on the ship's computing services into this little recorder. Theoretically.

"Thank you," I tell her.

"Of course. Also . . ." She hesitates. "I know Captain Io and First can be a bit . . . abrupt."

"Oh, First is very snuggly."

She smiles. "Just know that they're fair. They get the job done, and the captain's very strict, but they are fair. This is a good ship, a good crew."

"Are you telling me that I can have seconds at every meal? Because that will earn you lifelong loyalty."

"Absolutely," she says. "And don't let the captain bully you into thinking otherwise. Doctor's orders."

I give her a mock salute and then lug my stuff back to the room they say is mine. First things first, I check the life-support unit and the jetpack attachment and affix them to a hook near the door. All the tanks have been replenished, everything at max and ready to go. Nice. A full diagnostic proves all is well. Then I spread out my suit on the bed, meticulously going over every seam and line. Everything's still solid, and the suit should be able to seal correctly. I could toss myself outside again whenever I want to.

As I said, my suit's custom. When you scavenge alone, you learn that the two most important things to your survival are your suit and your ship. My ship's been breached. I can't afford to let my suit be anything less than perfect.

Not if I want my plan to work.

So, I hang it up beside the LifePack and check it one last time. Every seam. Every latch. Every connection.

What's mine is mine.

There's a small outer pocket on the chest of the suit, designed to be accessible while on black walks, just big enough for me to fit gloved fingers inside. I wonder if Rian or whoever scanned my suit checked the pockets. My odds are pretty even on that one. On the one hand, there wasn't much time, and digital scans are quick and noninvasive. On the other, Rian doesn't seem the type to miss anything.

Doesn't matter either way. I made sure it was empty before. Now I put the data recorder into my spacesuit's pocket instead, sealing it inside.

Last to be checked is my helmet. I run a quick analysis; the operational base of the suit is built into the inner shell of the headpiece. In the past two hours, someone's downloaded all the external communications I'd logged. There aren't many, I know that. Mostly me cursing and waiting to be rescued, a few logs from when I was recording what I'd found on the planet, data entries as I processed my finds and estimated value and buyers.

We're too far out to make any meaningful contact with someone in another system. Even if I had sent a message to someone from here, it would still be pinging around the galaxy. Data is slower than the speed of light, unless you have an intergalactic transmitter, and while the *Halifax* may be rich enough for that, I'm not.

I think about the scanner on the table in the med bay. I'd

bet real coin that scanner was used on my suit, checking for any trackers or outgoing signals. Probably Rian.

As if I'd make such a rookie mistake.

I see a flash out of the corner of my eye from the direction of the porthole. Oh, delightful—the crew Captain Ursula sent planetside is heading back up to the ship. I take the time to do one last check before I leave the room. I'm in no rush. It takes a while to dock a shuttle.

I get a little turned around but make it to the dock as the shuttle bay is almost fully repressurized. Both the captain and Rian wait at the bay doors; it's automatically locked until the pressure and O_2 are back in equilibrium with the rest of the ship. Ursula scowls. Rian smiles. Fifty-fifty, not bad.

"I can't wait to meet the rest of our crew!" I say, beaming at Ursula.

She almost looks complimented for a moment, then shifts to a glare. "*My* crew. Not ours."

"Not *yet*," I say, undeterred.

The bulkhead door hisses as it opens; the shuttle bay is safe for entry. Inside, the shuttle door also opens, and two suited people step out. I see the way the mirrored face shields turn from the captain to me. Pretty soon, the helmets are off, and both the crew members stare openly at me.

The person closest to me is a large woman with broad shoulders. Her suit's labeled with her surname—Yadav. I glance over at the other person, male, with a surname of Magnusson. Yadav has brown skin with deep warm undertones, and when she tugs down her skull cap, I see shining dark hair braided in a crown. Magnusson has chin-length blond hair, pale skin, and eyes narrowed in suspicion.

"Hi!" I say cheerily. "I'm your new crewmate!"

Magnusson gapes at me.

"Name's Ada Lamarr," I offer, sticking out my hand. He looks down at it and then to the captain, as if making sure I've not actually proffered a venomous snake.

Yadav removes her gloves and gives me her hand. "My name is Saraswati; do not call me Sara." Her voice is stern, but her smile is light. I note the way the second syllable of her name goes up a little when she pronounces it.

Magnusson doesn't offer me either a greeting or another name. "Why is she here?" He's looking at me but talking to the captain.

I guess he's not asking *how* I'm here because he already knows. The whole reason the *Halifax* delayed responding to my distress signal was they thought I was a sabotage attempt, and they probably rushed to get their crew on the ground first. My eyes flick to Magnusson's waist. He's carrying a blaster on his hip. Saraswati is too.

They expected trouble on land.

Good of them to be prepared; no fault in that. If I was paranoid like this crew, I would have assumed the worst. I wouldn't have waited hours and hours to make the rescue and almost leave the caller to die, but you know. Choices.

"So, how was it?" I ask Saraswati, the nicer of the two. "Did the entire world try to burn you up while also eating you?"

Saraswati snorts a laugh. "Yeah, pretty much." Her tone shifts a little as she turns to the captain. "Volatile conditions, as expected. But there were . . . complications. We recorded multiple significant seismic shifts, and the area forward of the wreckage shows—"

"We'll debrief once you've both had a chance to change," the captain says, cutting her off. "White, will you please escort our . . . refugee elsewhere."

"Where?" I ask eagerly, as if I've not been dismissed.

"Elsewhere," the captain growls.

Rian sweeps his hand toward the door, a smirk on his face. "I'm growing on her," I confide in a loud, carrying whisper. "The captain's going to hire me on properly any day now, I can tell."

I think the loud groan I hear behind me as I climb the steps out of the cargo hold is from the shuttle-bay door opening, but it could have been Ursula. Before I go back into the ship proper, I turn and wave. "Lovely to meet you, Saraswati!" I call. Magnusson looks up when Saraswati waves back, so I blow him a kiss that makes him scowl so hard, I'm surprised he can see under that furrowed brow.

6

Rian escorts me to the bridge.

"Ooh, this is new!" I say excitedly. "It's a real mark of your trust in me."

Rian neither confirms nor denies this. I take it as a win.

The bridge on *Halifax* is far more expansive than the little cockpit on *Glory*. I can fit a copilot and a navigator with me, but it's tight and there's a good chance someone's sitting on someone else in the tiny space. The *Halifax* is designed to easily fit a crew of at least four, with a few more spots left over if anyone wants a show. Saraswati and Magnusson aren't just shuttle crew; one of them is a nav, and one's an engineer, I'd bet coin on that.

Rian sits down at a table with an inlaid screen and gestures for me to sit opposite him. I swivel the chair on its base and plop down, my eyes bumping from the ostentatious captain's chair over to the lockbox built behind the main console, protected by a biometric scanner. It's shut and secure, I think, but I don't look at it too long. I don't want to call attention to it.

I fiddle with the earring in my left ear, a little silver stud. It's not just a metal decoration; it's got a pretty decent voice recorder in it, one not linked to any comm sys. I wear it always, a backup where I can record stuff offline. I could "accidentally" lose it here and let the audio pick up some of Rian's secrets . . .

No. Too risky. I'd have to retrieve it again to get the data off it. And if Rian finds it first, it'd give away the game. Still, looking around the bridge, I make a mental note to be better prepared next time.

If I had something valuable on board a ship like this, the lockbox here on the bridge is the most obvious place to put it.

I flip my gaze over to Rian, who's watching me as if I'm the most fascinating person in the room. I mean, true, there's only the two of us in here, but still. A girl likes to be appreciated.

"So, about your story," Rian says.

Great. This is more interrogation. One day, I'm gonna get him to trust me properly.

"I'm an open book." My smile is all teeth.

"So, in the three cycles you were on the planet—"

"Two," I say.

"Right, right. And how much metal were you able to scavenge?"

I laugh. "I didn't bother weighing it. But I got maybe a

third of my cargo bay filled? I was moving quick. Figured a wreck this size would draw some . . ." I rake my eyes over him. ". . . *unsavory* sorts here."

"Unsavory?" He cocks an eyebrow, a wry grin playing at his lips.

"Clearly the worst kind."

He holds my gaze just a beat too long, then he drops his eyes to the table. I can't see what the data screen set into the enameled surface shows; there's a privacy reflector on it. "About a third, though," he mutters, repeating what I told him.

"Give or take. I figured one or two more trips down would have done it. Had it all gone well, I might have left before you even got here."

He nods. His jaw is tight, and he doesn't look back up at me, despite the way he's got to feel my stare. "And you looted mostly . . ."

"Metal," I repeat. I don't bother hiding my impatience. I know what's in my cargo hold. Crumpled sheets of steel, copper wiring, alloys.

"About the hole that blew in the side of your ship," Rian starts. "You thought you ran your fuel too hot?"

I shove my frustration out of my nose in the form of an impatient sigh. I can see what he's doing. "Yeah, maybe." He opens his mouth, and I slam my palms on the table, forcing him to focus at me instead of the screen. "Fine. Look, I'll you the truth."

That eyebrow again. Ugh. Might as well get it over with.

"One of the containers at the wreck did have something of value," I start.

"Something not just scrap metal." He speaks with the tone of a man who already knows the truth.

"Yes," I growl. "I found a packer crate with half a dozen solar fuel rods."

His eyes widen at that. A nice little stumbling block for the man who thought he had me cornered.

"I know, I *know*, it's dumb to salvage fuel like that," I continue, plowing ahead. "And I checked it before I loaded it up."

"You took the whole crate?" he gasps.

"*No,* I'm not a fucking moron. I took *one.* And once I was back in orbit, I *very sensibly* checked it again and . . ." I shrug, as if what I'd found was obvious.

"And?" he prompts when I don't answer.

He's going to make me say it. "*And* it was cracked. A hairline fracture, barely visible."

Now his eyes are so wide, they might fall out of his sockets. Which would be a damn shame, because when he's not looking all gobsmacked, he's very hot. "But a broken solar fuel rod . . ." His voice trails off as he considers the implications.

Solar fuel rods are the most expensive part of keeping a ship running. Any looter who saw one would take one, even if the danger of a cracked fuel rod would be . . . catastrophic. And how could a fuel rod *not* be cracked if it were in a crash like the *Roundabout*'s? Still.

"Those things are fucking expensive," I mutter.

"Yes, but—"

"Well, I learned my lesson, didn't I?" I throw up my hands. I hate losing my cool like this, but damn. "As soon as I saw it was compromised—"

"That's one way to put it," he says under his breath.

"—I threw it out of the airlock. But it was too late."

Realization settles on him. The three-meter hole in the side of my ship. Right at the airlock. Rendering my ship breached and the cofferdam inaccessible.

"That's an . . . *impressive* way to destroy your own ship," Rian says finally.

"*Glory*'s not destroyed," I snap back.

He shrugs as if conceding the point, but it's hard to argue that a gaping hole isn't a legitimate concern.

Rian flicks the data screen built into the table, and the privacy filter fades. It takes me a second to register that I'm looking at the interior of my ship, caught through a drone lens. Rian sent out a cam to confirm my story. This was all recorded before. He's no doubt already viewed it at least once. I take one little nap, and he got busy spying on both my suit and my ship.

I shoot him a look that clearly says, *Really?*

He shrugs.

I mean, I get it. But my story is more airtight than my ship.

I made sure of that.

Rian taps a control. "Magnusson, can you confirm solar fuel on the *Roundabout* manifest?"

The crew member's voice is gravelly over the comm unit. "Stand by."

Rian smiles placidly at me, but I'm kind of pissed that he's so obvious about his line of questioning. Where is the respect here? I drop my eyes to the screen, watching the drone recording slowly pan about the bridge on *Glory* before drifting through the secure bulkhead door and down the main corridor, mimicking the path I'd taken before evacuating.

I know that ship backward and forward. Every rusty bolt, every frayed wire. She's mine.

And it guts me to see that wound on her side, so fresh and raw.

When I look up, Rian's eyes are softer. Kinder.

Shit.

I roll my shoulders back and stare at him, running my tongue on my teeth. I did not mean to let him see anything real. Before I can say something snappy, the comm crackles.

"*Roundabout* cargo logs confirm three full cases of solar fuel rods, contained within half-units."

Three? Damn. I should go steal some more.

Just not any of the cracked ones. Obviously.

"Do not think about going back for more," Rian says, eyeing me.

"I would never consider it," I say, aghast.

"Approximate location of those units would be . . ." Magnusson rattles off some number coordinates, and then Rian tells him to make note of possible danger should the remaining rods be cracked as well, for when Saraswati and Magnusson go back down.

I cross my arms over my chest as Rian disconnects the comm. "Told you."

Rian nods, still thinking.

Still trying to find a hole in my story.

"I was concerned that there was debris in the orbital field or something else that may pose a threat to the *Halifax*," Rian says, not quite meeting my eyes.

"Bullshit; you thought I faked my ship being damaged."

"Why didn't you seal your bulkhead? That would have maintained flight integrity and life support—"

"Yeah, if I still had power," I snap. "Turns out when you lose part of your portside hull, it takes out, you know. Power. Life support. A chance to survive."

Rian nods slowly.

"It's good to know that we don't need to worry about damage in the same way," Rian finally says. "I'll inform the captain that your ship lost viability due to . . ." He cleared his throat. "User error."

I stand up so abruptly that my seat goes swiveling. "User error?!" I shout. "I will have you know that I—"

"Took a cracked fuel rod to your own cargo bay and blew up your hull when you didn't evacuate it quickly enough?"

My mouth hangs open.

Rian stands, grinning, a gleam of triumph in his eyes. "Look, we all make mistakes," he allows.

"True," I grumble.

"It's just that my last mistake involved me staining my favorite shirt with hot sauce, and your last mistake led to—"

I punch him before he finishes, but all he does is laugh.

7

Rian takes me back to the mess hall.

"If I didn't know better, I'd think you were trying to seduce me," I say. When Rian's eyebrows shoot up, I add, "The way to my heart is *definitely* through my stomach."

His eyebrows go down, one side of his lips twitching up in a half-smile. "Noted. Well, the others will be here soon enough."

I go ahead and fill up my tray from the dispenser. The lentils have been replaced with some sort of goopy thing flecked with seeds and nuts that tastes almost like vanilla. There are dehydrated slices of a yellow fruit mixed in, and beside that are protein balls that have, blessedly, been seasoned with something spicy enough to make me appreciate the goop.

"You guys have variety," I say, shooting him a grin. Rian's not taken a tray for himself. I wonder if I can get his serving later.

"I'm guessing your team found out that there are some complications planetside that you didn't expect," I say, pointing a spoon at Rian before turning it back to the goop.

"We have extensive scans," he replies. "We didn't send Yadav and Magnusson down blind."

I nod, mouth full, then swallow. "Scans are nothing compared to boots on the ground."

"True," he allows. "Is that stuff really that good?"

"Mm-hm."

He gives me a doubtful look.

"But see," I say, skewering a protein ball, "the thing is, *Roundabout* didn't crash right."

"There's a right way to crash?"

Damn, these things are chewy. "Obviously. If a ship breaks down in space, that's the best option."

"Didn't work so well for you."

"Hey, I'm here, aren't I? Despite 'user error.'"

I glare. He smirks.

"Besides," I continue, "we're talking about a scavenger's point of view. A ghost ship floating in space? Creepy as fuck, but easy to loot."

Rian snorts.

"Next, you want an easy slide on ground. If the crew has control of the ship and if the engine's not completely shot, then if you have to crash, you can aim it." I hold my spoon out at an angle, pointed to my tray, then rush the spoon down so it slides into the goop. "*Roundabout* didn't do that. It basically hit that planet like a dart. Which complicates looting."

Rian doesn't say anything; he just sits there, eyes zeroed in on me as if he's seeing *everything* I'm not saying. And I'm not saying a lot. That makes me nervous, which makes me want to talk more, so I stuff another protein ball in my mouth. I don't really want him to think too much about how the crash happened; I want him to consider how much he needs me planetside. I'm getting itchy, cooped up on this ship.

The door slides open, and the rest of the crew—minus First—enter.

"So, *Roundabout* hit nose first and broke into two pieces," I continue, focusing on Rian. "They crashed wrong."

"Damn right they did," Saraswati says. Magnusson and the captain head over to the food dispenser. Nandina cuts in front of them when the captain motions for her to, and she takes two trays—one for her and the other, presumably, for First, who must be on some sort of duty right now. She leaves with a little smile to me.

"You saw." I point my spoon at Saraswati. "It's a mess down there. Which, actually, works to my benefit. Scrap's easier to pick up when it's already broken off a ship."

Magnusson growls and thumps his tray down on the table. The captain sits down beside Rian.

"The fact that the ship is broken is bad enough," Saraswati says. "But the nose hit a ridge, and—"

"We are not discussing the mission in front of a civilian," Captain Ursula says coldly.

"I'm not a *civilian*," I say, rolling my eyes. "Think of me as a consultant."

"You're a refugee. Only." She glares at me, which is dumb, because she could be using that energy to eat instead. I demonstrate the more practical use of time, which just seems to make her glare harder, if possible.

"Okay, then," I say. "Small talk. Who's from Earth?" I raise my left hand while scraping the tray with the spoon in my right hand.

They all know I mean Sol-Earth. The planet that revolves around a sun that was once thought to be the *only* sun. The Earth where homo sapiens came from. All the other planets—Centauri-Earth, Rigel-Earth, Gliese-Earth—they're the colonies built later. But if anyone asks about Earth without putting a different star's name in front of it, they're talking about the original.

Surprisingly, it's Magnusson who tentatively raises his hand, as if unsure that's what he should do. "Oh, really?" I say, turning my attention to him. "Which part?"

"Iceland."

I cringe, and he nods. Iceland's seismic activity has only gotten worse lately; there are stabilizers, but it's been increasingly difficult to sell the island as a tourist location after one too many buildings collapsed. Plus, it didn't exactly have the historical and architectural draw like other places—Iceland sold its landscape, but the continental rift kept underselling it. I suppose that's why he's here, in space. Easier to make a living on a ship than a dying island.

"I was born near Yellowstone," I say. Now it's his turn to cringe. That volcano was dormant for a millennium or more, but when it blew, it ripped apart North America. "My family immigrated to Malta the year before." At least we had warning that it was going to blow, and the smog eaters kept the smoke from changing the atmosphere to a catastrophic level.

"Malta's nice," Magnusson says.

"I did tours," I say.

Magnusson nods stoically, but somehow I don't mind the blank face now that I know where it comes from. Malta's had its share of issues as well. Formerly the location of the global government, the only thing bringing in funds now are the tourists looking for a bit of history. At least we have some truly ancient digs and locations to go alongside the beaches that are still pristine—although the only thing that keeps the ocean water blue surrounding the island nation is liberal application of dye and a perimeter of cleaner drones blocking trash from washing up.

That's what Earth is now. Little bubbles of tourist locations that hide the last dying gasps of a world that's been polluted to death.

"If you're from Earth," Rian says, "do you know Jane Irwin?"

Three things happen at once.

1. Magnusson's head snaps up to Rian, shock evident on his face for a split second before he grabs his cup and chugs some water.

2. Rian doesn't notice this because he's too busy watching me.

3. I keep my face so perfectly regulated that I am actually a hundred percent certain he doesn't see even a flicker of recognition. There's another test I've passed.

I roll my eyes. "Why do people assume everyone on Earth knows each other? Just because our population is down and our cities are bubbled doesn't mean Earth isn't an *entire planet* of people. There are *billions* of people still on Earth."

"Oh, uh, yeah. I guess," Rian says, flustered. A rare misstep. He thought he had me.

"My parents transferred to Centauri-Earth before I was born," Saraswati offers. "I've always wanted to visit Agra."

Centauri-Earth. That explains why she's so nice. Closest to Earth, the first settled world outside the original. Half the people on Centauri-Earth claim to be descended from the original colonists, which is statistically unlikely but pretty decent for the tourism trade with so many people spending buckets on pilgrimages to the home world.

"I've been to Agra." Both my and Saraswati's eyes widen a little as the captain speaks. "I did a tour of the Old World after I graduated officer academy." Her eyes grow a little distant. "We spent so many days at sea."

"Did you see the oceans?" I ask.

"Oh, of course not. But the landhoppers brought us to the cities on the tour."

She was on one of those fancy cruises, then. Every port-hole is actually a digi-screen, displaying idyllic views and blocking out the brown, dead sea water. Landhoppers carry guests directly into the tourist bubbles. *It's the only way to view Earth now,* a tourist once told me. To see only the parts that are clean and fake.

"I'm going to guess you're from Gliese-Earth?" I say.

For the first time ever, Ursula looks at me as if she's impressed. Last world to be colonized, although it's had a few centuries to grow. I've only been there a handful of times. It's a pain in the ass to get to, which may be why it has a growing movement of people who want to withdraw the world from the United Galactic System. I don't care enough to keep up with the politics of it all, but Gliese-Earth basically claims too much of its money goes to the other worlds and they don't get enough benefits from the union. But Gliese-Earth absolutely would produce someone who thinks they saw all Earth has to offer from a view in a landhopper. It pains me to think of my new best friend that way, but it's pretty obvious Ursula was raised to think of my planet as a commodity to consume, a box to tick off.

I glance at Rian, the only other person in room. He smiles without answering the implied question. I'm going to guess he's from Rigel-Earth. He seems like the kind of guy who comes from Rigel-Earth. A world full of pretentious assholes. It has the best portal systems, the best natural resources, the best world design, and the taxes and regulations to keep riffraff like me off-world. If Gliese-Earth thinks of my home as a product to consume, Rigel-Earth only thinks of it as a burdensome charity case. Most people who have never had to look at the golden safety net underneath them to know they'll be fine if they fall have no concept whatsoever that poverty isn't a matter of bad choices and poor planning.

But if Rian's from Rigel-Earth, that makes me want to punch him, and he's got too pretty of a face for me to actually want to smash it in, even when he says "user error," so I tell myself he's from Gliese-Earth and his sharp eyes that always seem to stare right into the heart of me are a result of protesting the government's bid for secession and not because he's actually that intelligent.

"So, anyway," I say. "About the *Roundabout*."

"We're not discussing the mission," Captain Ursula says instantly.

"Well, *they* can't discuss the ship," I say. "But I can. And maybe something I say will help."

I clock the way Magnusson glances at Ursula. I'm right. They know it. Whew, do I love it when that happens.

"I'm assuming from all this secrecy that you guys are looking for something specific on board the *Roundabout*. Let me go ahead and answer the question I'm certain you're thinking," I add, pointedly looking at Magnusson and Saraswati. "All I was able to do was make one load of scrap metal, all of it sheets of wall paneling, pretty much."

"And a cracked solar fuel rod," Rian mutters.

I glare at him. "None of which I'm assuming you were looking for in the first place."

Magnusson stuffs his spoon in his mouth, but Saraswati gives me a little nod, confirming what I already know.

"So, where did you guys explore—the forward or the aft part of the ship?"

Magnusson glances at Ursula. Saraswati just answers me. "Forward."

"Yadav!" the captain says.

Saraswati shrugs. "Fine, reprimand me, but if we're going to get the—"

I pretend not to care, but come on, how can I not?

Saraswati's mouth snaps shut. She doesn't say *what* they're looking for. Instead, she says, "If we have any hope of finding the *items*, we can use all the help we can get. Especially after—"

"Enough!" Captain Ursula roars, throwing her spoon on the table. "Yadav, you're walking a dangerous line right now."

"Hey, I don't want to get people in trouble." I hold both my hands up in a show of peace. "If Saraswati can't talk, let me."

"You certainly love to do that," Magnusson grumbles.

I ignore him because I'm the bigger person. "I'm guessing that whatever you're looking for isn't that large. It's at least something that two people working together can pick up." I gesture at the two ground-crew members. The shuttle they rode in on wasn't big enough for a hover lift, nor did it have the cargo room to store anything too sizable. "Plus if you're talking about the forward . . . the nose of that ship is in a rift. With lava at the bottom. And on not exactly stable ground."

I think for a moment, tapping my chin. "Yeah, either way, you're going to need me."

Ursula cocks an eyebrow at me. "What makes you presume so?"

So uptight, this one. "Right, so, option one is that whatever thing you're looking for, it's inside the ship still, but it's not safe to reach. Ground's unstable, magma's trying to break through the cracks in the earth to burn it all up, et cetera, et cetera." I don't pause in my speech, but I can tell from the others, this isn't right. Saraswati's frowning, and Magnusson is grinning. "Option B is—"

"Two," Rian says. "Option two."

"Option two is whatever *items* you're looking for, they've scattered. The ship didn't just wreck; it broke apart and partially exploded on impact. Which created a scatter zone of the items that got tossed outside on the surface."

Magnusson's grin fades, and Saraswati leans forward. This is definitely what happened.

"Which creates a bigger problem, really," I continue. "If whatever you're looking for was inside the ship, it would be somewhat protected. But outside the ship? The volatile conditions of the planet make it at risk of being destroyed or lost forever."

I sit back, done.

"I thought you said you were only scavenging from the aft end of the ship," the captain says.

"Yeah, because the forward was a shit hole and not worth my time. Good thing for you, I've reconsidered."

"Reconsidered?" Magnusson says.

"I'll get your item for you. Sorry, I mean item*s*." Plural.

"You?" Ursula scoffs. "Magnusson and Yadav are experts, and—"

"And we can't get it," Saraswati says, leaning over the table to look at the captain. "I already told you, I will not risk my life for this mission. It's not worth it."

I wonder how much they're paying her.

"You've only been down once," the captain says. "I'm sure with some additional analysis and—"

"And God's grace there's not another earthquake," Magnusson mumbles.

I bite back a smirk. There's a ticking time bomb to getting at least one of the items—if an earthquake rattles the surface around too hard or a volcano burps up some lava, it could be lost. For once, a short time frame is working in my favor.

Blink.

"How do you know you can get it?" Rian asks. His voice is soft, but it slices through the lingering questions and tension at the table.

There it is, I think. *Finally.*

All eyes to me.

But my gaze is locked on his.

I slide my empty tray over and prop my elbows on the table, hands under my chin as I smile up at him. "Because," I drawl, "I *never* know when to give up."

8

Rian's not even gotten a tray of food, but he stands up anyway, offering me his arm like we're in some period drama feed and not . . . here. I take his elbow anyway, because *obviously*, and we swan out of there.

"Do you actually think you can get something Yadav and Magnusson cannot?" he asks me. Just idle conversation.

"Yes."

"Confident."

"Experienced."

"It seems that way." He leads me forward, away from the bunks. My skin zings with anticipation. There seems to be possibility weaving around us like smoke. And where there's smoke, well . . . you know the rest. I slip my arm out of his, slowing down a little so I can better look at my surroundings. This is a part of the ship I don't think I'd be allowed to see without him.

"So, what's your role here?" I say. "Captain, First, the doc—those are standard on a ship. And Saraswati and Magnusson are clearly your muscle."

"Can't I be the muscle, too?" Rian smirks, but here's the thing. I was just touching his arm, and it is solid. The man definitely doesn't spend all his time on spaceships letting his muscles atrophy and taking bio-enhancer supplements to make up for zero-g. I mean, I'm not wormy-armed myself, and I can lug up the scrap on the hover as well as anyone, I guess, but like . . . that arm was nice; that's what I'm saying.

Rian takes mercy on me, as if he can guess how my mind went spinning sideways. "I'm the brains," he says.

"Oh."

"You sound surprised."

I smile beatifically up at him. That's what he gets for having good arms. And for saying my problems were "user error." And for probably being from Rigel-Earth, despite my best attempts to pretend otherwise. I mean, I definitely get smug when I'm right, but the difference is I *know* I'm right, and so the fact that he's smug when I don't know if he's actually right is infuriating.

He stops outside a door with a bioscanner lock, and he leans forward, letting his eye be scanned. He's put his body in front of the door, but I notice he slides his finger over a print-scanner bar. Double security, all linked to him. The door zings open.

This isn't a bunk room, but it's got the homey feel of one. There's tea with a little steam wafting off it on the ta-ble, next to several data pads, scanners, and one actual paper notebook that's firmly closed. I long to touch it—real paper? I've not felt that thin, smooth stuff in . . . years, I think. Not since I left home.

Rian activates a holo projector in the center of the room. A scan of the *Roundabout* illuminates, twirling slowly around. As I watch, it breaks apart into two pieces, small blocks representing the debris scattering around. The holo settles onto a projection of the crash site on the planet surface, the tail end near me, the nose pointing straight down in a rift.

I shift closer to Rian, watching the projection. High-tech scans. It all matches what I saw on the surface. They used drones, I suppose, just like they did on *Glory*.

But there's some detail missing, especially in the smaller items, especially near the bottom of the rift.

"Heat kept your drones from scanning," I comment, pointing near the bottom of the projection. It's nothing but fuzzy light.

"There are lava flows," Rian says. "Hot enough to disrupt imagery."

"If it's hot enough to mess up digital images, it's too hot to get anything down there," I say. "Hope the thing you want isn't on one of those ledges." I point to the projection of boxes that have settled along the outcroppings of rock above the lava river.

"It is," Rian says grimly. "Yadav confirmed."

"Thermal protection at least?" That would be the only

way the item inside isn't melted from the radiant heat of the lava. Rian confirms, detailing not just the box's material but also its dimensions.

Not the contents, though.

That's okay. I already know. Not that he knows I know, but . . . you know.

"Right, so, whatever's inside the box is safe," I start.

"For now," Rian adds grimly.

And there's the rub. See, before, when the only thing spurring them to action was my distress signal and their paranoia thinking I was laying a trap rather than dying, they thought the biggest threat to retrieving the box's contents would be someone like me.

They forgot about the planet itself.

Constant earthquakes, volcanos rumbling, tectonic plates shifting about, rivers made of literal molten rock, violent geysers spraying out debris . . . not exactly a safe place to store something valuable.

This thermal- and impact-protected case is fine for now, resting on a ledge a few meters above a lava flow. But one violent shrug of the protoplanet's shoulders, and that box is going on a river ride made of fire and not even its thermal protections will help.

I lean back, looking at the holographic projection. "You're going to hire me," I say confidently. I turn to him. "We should call the captain, negotiate terms."

"The captain doesn't make those decisions."

How hot is he when he says that? Just all casual, like it's not a big deal.

"You do?" I say, already knowing the answer from the way he stands there, feet rooted, body relaxed. Eyes sharp as splintered glass.

"She's in charge of the ship. I'm in charge of the mission."

Explains the room, then. This is a war room, and it's just for him. A delicious shiver tickles my spine. I wonder if the rest of the crew have been in here. Probably. A little pang of disappointment at that.

But Rian knows what it means to show me this, I think. *And he's too smart not to have an angle.*

I've got to be careful now. Which is a problem, because the idea that Rian's playing me just as much as I'm playing him?

Like I said, hot.

I want to pin him down on top of the flat base of the holo projector and get him to tell me all those secrets behind those eyes of his. He's after the box—does he know what's inside of it the way I know what's inside of it? Does he know what it all means? What it's worth?

Everything, I think. *It's worth everything.*

"Climbing down won't work," I say, scrutinizing the image. "Too slow, and you'd be exposed to the heat too long."

"Temperatures are indeed high enough to compromise

the integrity of our protective gear if the exposure is too long."

"Drones get knocked off by radiant heat waves," I continue, thinking aloud. "Dropping a hook down is too risky."

Rian motions for me to come closer and get a different angle. The box is right on the lip of the ledge, about a quarter of it actually hanging off the exposed side. It's a miracle it hasn't already fallen over the side.

"I saw your suits," I say.

Rian's face flashes in surprise, and that makes me trill with eagerness. I like startling a man who thinks he knows everything. He's got every step planned, but if I can keep him on his toes, he might just stumble.

"You've got space jets," I continue, granting him mercy by providing an explanation. "CO_2 cartridges?"

He nods. Lightweight, efficient, easy to recharge. Most suits are only equipped with space jets.

"That'll maneuver you in low gravity. But I have a jaxon jet."

"I know," he says, his voice low, all personal. I can't help but raise an eyebrow at him. I mean . . . he definitely didn't miss that detail when he inspected my suit.

"You kept going on about it," he adds, smirking.

Oh. Right. I'd forgotten about that.

He hadn't.

But I can see those tiny gears working behind those

clear-as-carbonglass eyes. My jaxon jet is the only possible thing that can help him get the loot. Nothing else on the *Halifax* has the maneuverability and control that my jets have.

He turns to look at the holo projection again, considering. "It'd be dangerous," he says to the shimmering light. "At least the last ten meters would all be manual—the heat messes with the sensors. You'd have to have absolute control."

"Don't worry; I like being in control."

Rian raises his eyebrows. I see the moment it settles in his mind, that we're in a dark room, alone, together, nothing between us but the plans that may mean my horrifyingly gruesome death. So romantic.

"My suit's custom-fitted, and I know my jetpack. I can get down to that box, grab it, and get out. Or you can faff around and wait for a quake to knock it into the lava. It doesn't really matter to me," I lie.

And then, just because I can, I tell him the truth. "I'm the only hope you have."

9

'm not doing it for free, obviously.

Rian told me a price that was generous for me to give it an honest try, and he offered to double it if I actually succeeded. So, the next morning, I trot my suited self down to the shuttle bay.

I did a check in my room, even though thincraft suits are pretty failsafe. My LifePack is fully charged and every port's connected. My boots are sealed. I even inspected my helmet; my visor is dual-layered with all my controls and comms there. I may take risks, but never with a suit that's not tops.

Magnusson and Saraswati are already there, and before I reach the shuttle, Rian shows up. Also suited. So, the boss is coming with us this time. Just to keep an eye on me. I'm flattered, really.

"Suit check," Saraswati tells me as I put on my helmet and lock it into place.

"It's self-contained," I try to tell her, but she ignores me. She manually checks all the connections, ensures everything's sealed, double- and triple-checking the gauges to make sure I'm full up on the essentials. She's focused, going over a mental checklist, seeing each individual point rather than the suit as a whole.

"See? It's fine. Want me to check you?" I ask, grinning.

There's just a flicker, the barest shuttering of her emotions, and then she grins too. "No, that's okay. Magnusson?"

Magnusson checks her suit, then she checks his. They're both still wearing blasters.

I try not to let that bother me.

I don't offer to check Rian's suit. Magnusson does it. And when I stomp up the ramp into the shuttle and Saraswati shoots me a concerned look, I don't try to mask what I'm actually thinking.

I'm not being fair. And I know it.

But still.

Stings a little.

Magnusson takes the pilot position; Saraswati sits as co-pilot. Rian and I strap in behind them on jump seats, little pulldown metal chairs that seem to have been added as an afterthought. We face each other, our knees bumping together. The captain sees us off, then seals the shuttle bay. It takes time to decompress the bay, and the exterior hatch won't open until that's done.

Not unless someone pushes the big red emergency button.

That would pop off the bay door and suck us out into space in a wild burst of explosive decompression.

Not that I would do that.

Would be kind of neat to see it happen, though.

But I wouldn't. Really. Even I'm not so reckless to toss a whole ship out into space without proper decompression. I'm just a curious sort, that's all.

No one talks once the shuttle is out in the black. Magnusson and Saraswati are focused on maneuvering the shuttle down to the planet, and Rian's not looking at me. I try to catch his attention, but he's got his eyes shut. I can just barely hear his breathing over the comm channel we're all sharing in our helmets.

He looks a little sick. Which is kind of hilarious, considering. Never thought he'd be the nervous flyer of the group.

Magnusson is a good pilot. There's not much atmosphere on this protoplanet—certainly not enough for humans to dare take off their helmets—but there's some nitrogen and methane at least, enough for the shuttle to adjust slightly when we hit it. I was right. Give it an eon or so, and this may be a whole new world, with breathable air, oceans, flora and fauna. Maybe even people, the curious sort. Like me.

Not now, though.

Now, it's just a barely crusted-over lava field waiting to kill us all.

Saraswati points out a landing spot about a klick away from the crash site, clear and flat. It's made of cooled lava, and while this area is absolutely volatile, it's not a bad place to park, all things considered.

Before we reach it, we fly over the wreckage. From up high, the lava river shines vividly, bright red with flecks of orange cutting through the burnt-black rock. I can see the long line of debris and scorch marks that lead to the crash, but my eyes are drawn to brighter colors under the cracked, black earth, a stark contrast. People think of living worlds as blue and green, cloudy atmospheres over water and plants. But there's life here, too, or the potential for it, at least. That molten rock may as well be placenta.

Once we're landed, Rian tosses off his harness and stands. "I'll stay with the ship," he says so quickly that at first I wonder if maybe he's afraid of the planet, not flight. But the others seem to take this in stride. They must have discussed everything before. Without me.

Saraswati motions for me to follow her and Magnusson. "We'll get visuals first," she says. "You were already on the crash site. Did you go to the bridge?"

I shake my head, but the helmets don't exactly convey emotion. "No," I say over the comm sys.

"This way." Magnusson takes the lead.

Despite being a baby planet with little atmosphere, this

world does at least have gravity, which slows us down considerably. I notice stakes imbedded in the ground along our route, and Saraswati has a seismic reader in her hand. They were busy yesterday.

"Level two coming in," Saraswati says, and a moment later, the earth trembles. I've never seen anything like it. Back home, on Earth, there's water—a whole ocean—surrounding my island nation. Sometimes, I'll watch the waves crest and fall. But I never thought I'd see *earth* do the same, a solid mass that is supposed to be flat and stay flat rippling up and shuddering like liquid.

Magnusson curses. He's quite good at it. I learn a few new words.

He's not upset at the earthquake; all things considered, it was a mild one, if freaky. In front of us, though, we see the nose of the crashed ship dip a little, sliding farther down into the crevice of cracked rock. I don't think any of them care about the ship, but if the box they want is inside the rift, then the ship crashing down into it will knock it well out of reach.

I add that to my list of things that could go wrong and kill me:

1. The radiant heat of the lava river at the bottom of the ridge could knock out my sensors and make me crash into it, burning me alive. It's unlikely but possible.

2. Getting the box and then dropping it may make the others mad enough to be a problem. Again, unlikely, but they already don't trust me, and if I'm the cause of them losing this precious top-secret prize . . . I don't think it would make any of them happy, at least.

3. All my other plans could go awry, and then they'd *definitely* kill me. Or at least throw me in a brig and let a judge kill me a little more "fairly." You can never tell with these law-abiding types.

And now, also:

4. The forward part of the ship could crash through the rift and squish me into the ledge, into the lava river, or a combination of the two, which is less than ideal.

I stand with my hands on my hips when we reach the rift, looking down, and it probably makes them think I'm considering odds or something, but I'm appreciating the scenery. Rather than a smooth, sheared break, the rock that's split apart looks as if it were made of vertical pillars stacked together, cracking apart like candle ice. It's created a series of step-like platforms all along the face, many with debris, some sloping down or crumbling. I'm not sure what the integrity of this rock is. The ground under my feet feels solid, but I'm pretty sure the *Roundabout* felt solid before it exploded too.

"It's about eighty meters," Magnusson says.

I scan the rift with my helmet's sensors. Eighty-one point ten meters. There's a significant drop in temperature between the top and the bottom; standing a meter away from the edge shows only a negligent difference in ambient temperature; leaning over the edge and facing down notice-ably shifts the gauge.

Once we reach the splintered nose of the ship, Saraswati stays outside, focused on the seismic reader.

"We're not going to go all the way in," Magnusson says. "It's already not stable, and I'm just trying to get you a good visual from this side. It's how I found the box in the first place."

The *Roundabout* hit the planet at a sharp angle that forced the nose to snap off, leaving the back end to skid along the edge of the surface. There's a kilometer-long track of metal scarring the ground, and the bridge tips along the edge of the cliff at such an angle that the open wound of the ship faces us. We don't need a door to enter; the side wall has been worn away in the worst type of road rash.

I pause, eyes tracing the damage. With one side burned off and the different levels of the ship exposed in an unin-tended cross-section, it feels as if I'm looking at the bones of a half-rotted corpse. Wiring dangles from the top and sides, veins cut off from the main core with nothing left to bleed, not even sparks. This ship is four times the size of the *Halifax* at least, and a monster compared to my *Glory*. It was never meant to have its skin peeled back, its weaknesses exposed.

Glory was breached, and not a one of them batted an eye. The old and the weak are supposed to die.

But this is a ship cut down in its prime. An unwanted reminder of fragility and mortality. That merits some reverence.

"Come on," Magnusson says impatiently.

Maybe I'm the only philosophical one here.

I bound up to him, using a hunk of twisted metal to leverage my way up to what should be the second floor. We stick close to the edge, careful to not fall out the exposed side, but with enough room, I note, that we could launch ourselves back to land if another seismic shift happens and the ship starts to fall.

It doesn't take long to get to the bridge, and stepping through the mangled wall is easy enough, even if I have to be careful to keep my suit from sharp edges. The carbon-glass viewport is completely shattered, bits of debris crunching under the solid soles of my reinforced boots.

I linger at one of the crew's seats. The navigation console in front of the chair is pristine, not a mark on it. The harness attached to the metal frame of the seat dangles loosely, the metal latches gleaming in the dim light.

Wherever the crew had been when the *Roundabout* crashed, it wasn't here.

When I turn around, Magnusson is staring at me, eyes narrowed. Before I can do anything, he raises his gloved hands and makes a gesture I know well.

You sign?

In space, you can't always count on comms. Things break or malfunction or glitch, and when communication can mean life or death, you learn to have backups. Stuff that doesn't rely on tech. Everyone who's done enough black walks knows the basics of sign language.

But Magnusson isn't signing now because of broken tech.

Yes, I sign back.

He knows that Rian is listening to our comms. He knows that anything we say in our suits will be analyzed, recorded.

Possibly used against us.

You a friend of Jane? Magnusson signs. His eyes are sharply focused on my face, not my hands, and he almost misses my answer:

I've worked with her before. Jane is not a person. Jane is a code word—one that I clocked Magnusson recognizing—to indicate a pro-Earth movement. They're not a bad lot, if misguided. Ideals will do that. Nobility only goes so far, and it certainly doesn't pay the bills. Any job I do with them begins and ends with a paycheck. *I've worked with a lot of different people.*

Magnusson's jaw is so tight, I can see it tense even from here. *You working with them now?*

I shrug. *I work for whoever pays me best. Currently, that's Rian.*

You ever work for the Jarra? It takes him longer to finger-spell that name, each letter carefully formed by his gloved hands.

My answer is swift and clear. *No. Never.* I make a sharp gesture with my hand, a slash through the dead air, to emphasize my words.

I may chase coins, but even I have standards. I've crossed paths with the Jarra before, enough to know that if I ever shake my hands with someone from that organization, my palms will come away bloody. They're freedom fighters, emphasis on the *fighter* part. They want Earth separated from all the colonial planets, from tourism to intergalactic governmental aid, and they don't care who they hurt in the process. I don't have the bank account to give me morals, but I've never been low enough to cross that line.

Magnusson still doesn't trust me. That much is clear. But at least my rebuttal of the Jarra has met with his approval.

Is that what this is? I ask, gesturing toward the broken bridge, but I mean more than just the crashed ship; I mean the missing items they've all crossed the galaxy to get. *Something the Jarra want?*

He hesitates before answering. He still doesn't trust me. In the end, he just shrugs. I'm not sure if that means he doesn't know if the Jarra did this, or if he doesn't know if he can trust me enough to tell me.

"This is where the box was supposed to be," Magnusson says over the comms, pointing to a security wall that's been blown apart by the impact. I guess my silent interrogation is over, and now it's time to get to work. He turns, indicating the broken, twisted frame that once held the viewport. "That's where it is."

I step closer, moving carefully. From here, I get a view of just how wide the rift is. How deep.

And how precariously small and close to the edge the box is.

The port view window smashed on impact, contents spewing through the opening. When the *Roundabout* vomited up whatever wasn't strapped down in the bridge, a good chunk of it probably fell straight down into the lava. Smaller items are scattered along the broken edges of the rift.

The box is made of white, reflective material, and from here I can see the silvery reinforcements around the edge.

"You *sure* whatever's inside isn't melted or broken?" I ask. No point risking my life for something that's already gone.

"There's some pretty heavy padding and insulation." Rian answers from the comm unit, not Magnusson. "The actual object inside is no bigger than your palm. I've not been able to get a proper scan in, but the chances are legitimately good."

"For now," Saraswati says. "Eyes up. Incoming level three."

Magnusson and I brace against whatever we can reach that's bolted to the floor of the bridge. I grab the nav console; he hangs on to the captain's seat, legs spread wide. This was a slightly more violent quake, and the fact that I'm deeply aware of being on a ship hanging halfway over a high rift that ends in lava makes it worse, but thankfully, it ends quickly.

The whole time, Magnusson's eyes are on the box.

"Still think you can get it?" Magnusson asks. He's not being snide; he sounds truly curious.

I nod silently.

He moves closer, his voice dropping. "Listen, you don't have to prove anything. You're a scavenger, and you've got experience, but there's no point risking your life for something just to prove a point."

We're on a public comm channel, and even if Rian's in the ship and Saraswati's outside, they can still hear him. Can still hear my reply. Kind of wish he'd signed all that rather than voiced it.

"That's not what this is," I say.

"But—"

I turn back to look at the box. This is going to be complicated; no point pretending otherwise. I can't even lie to myself on this one.

"How?" Magnusson says in a whisper, like he barely dares to ask the question.

"Here's how," I say. "One goal. Full speed until you get it. It's the only way."

10

Before Magnusson and I leave the broken remains of the bridge, Rian's voice fills the comm unit. "Yadav, Magnusson, carry on with your mission. And if you find the recorder box, grab that, too."

The recorder box transcribes all the data of a flight mission, a digital record of everything that happens. It could tell them why the ship crashed in the first place. If they find it, and if it's not too damaged. The box is supposed to be on the bridge, near the captain's console, but it's not there now, so it may already be burned up by now. *Anything* could have happened to it.

"I'm switching Lamarr to a private channel so your chatter doesn't distract her," Rian continues.

"Before you go private," Magnusson starts, but I can't hear him because Saraswati speaks at the same time, their voices clattering together.

Rian cuts through. "One at a time."

"Yadav, you go," Magnusson says. He gestures for me to start climbing down out of the ship. We go slowly around the ragged metal, then reach the twisted steps we took to get up to this level.

"I said before—this job isn't worth risking your life over," Saraswati says. I can see her below, on the ground, her helmet tilted up to us. Worry leaks into her voice, crackling through the communication channel.

"Actually, you said the job isn't worth *your* life," I say. "Mine, on the other hand?" I jump down out of the ship, landing on the slick obsidian rocks below, my boots skidding. I manage to remain upright, even as Saraswati rushes over to help me. At least Rian isn't here to see that less-than-graceful descent. Magnusson takes his time climbing out of the rubble, and even though he doesn't say anything, I can feel his aggravation at me radiating over comm.

"No one's going to die," Rian interrupts. "Switch channels." There's a slight hiss in my ear, and then it's just Rian. "Hey, Ada."

Oh, it's Ada now, not Lamarr. And don't think I missed that "mission" bit from before everyone got all squeamish about death—the other two are now searching for the second "item" they've been sent to find. Never waste a moment. Well, I can't blame them. The nose of this ship is going to fall into the rift any minute—if they think something else they need is hidden in the rubble, best find it before the whole bridge flops into the lava river.

"Yadav is right," Rian continues, "you don't have to try for this."

"So, you don't think the box is worth it either?" I quip.

Rian's silent for a beat too long. And in that space, I know: He *does* think this is life-or-death. "You don't have to do it," he says finally, which is not an answer to my question.

"It's fine, it's fine," I say. "You guys are all extremely dramatic; has anyone told you that? It's a *box*. I can handle a box." I check my jetpack levels, analyzing how much thrust I'm going to need, inputting the variable heat radiance I'm expecting when I go down. "You don't want to admit it, but this job is just scavenging. You've fancied it up, but it's still looting."

"And you're good at looting."

"The best," I say. "When a ship like this crashes, there's a lot to take. You have to train your eyes. Can't take everything, not at once."

"I heard you. One goal."

"Full speed," I add.

"That really doesn't sound like good logic, and—"

I boot my jetpack on and shoot straight up.

"Okay, we're doing this," Rian mutters.

I adjust my helmet. Like I said, everything here's custom-fitted to me and what I need. I may cheap out on some things but *never* on my suit. Rian has some idea of this. He had to have been the one to scan my suit in the med-bay locker, downloading all the info and specs. But there's a difference between knowing what an object can do and seeing it.

I swoop over the ridge, analyzing the heat differential. A jetpack that operates on land through hot air propulsion is going to fuck up over a lava river. That's why jaxon fuel makes a difference here. Thermodynamics still apply, but the cold burn is more stable.

I came prepared.

Full speed, I think, shooting straight down toward the lava. Meters flick by in seconds. Twenty down, forty, sixty.

One goal, I think, veering close to the ridge side.

My targeting array is focused on the box, locked in with a constant stream of data scrolling through the left side of my vision, blocking out much of the lava stream. Thankfully. Don't really want to be reminded of how if my jets fail, I burn alive. No suit I've ever seen can withstand a dip in a river like that.

I flex my fingers. My gloves are thincraft too but not thin enough. Not like real skin. That can't be helped, though. Not only because there's no oxygen on this planet, and taking the gloves off means breaching the suit; the thincraft material is doing what it can to protect me from the heat.

My eyes flick to the temperature gauge. The lava itself is more than a thousand degrees centigrade, but the box is more than ten meters above the flow, putting thermal flux still in the danger zone. I have to be quick about this. I'm sweating, and it's already distracting, not just because salt stings my eyes but because I can feel my whole body slick with it, too much for the inner liner to wick away, which means it's getting into dangerous levels for both my body and the suit to operate properly.

But it's so *close*.

An insulated lockbox, teetering on the edge of a mini-cliff in the rift's sheer side. I jet closer, closer.

Almost—

"Ada," Rian starts.

"Shut up," I grit out. I can't afford any distraction. I don't need a pep talk or a warning.

I just need to reach—

Another quake. I don't feel it, suspended by the jetpack as I am, but I *see* it. The pillars of stone tremble and slide, a whole chunk of the opposite rock face falling down. I just register it out of the corner of my eye as my fingertips touch the edge of the box. The quake shifts—this time in my favor—the box sliding into my grip. I seize it and curl my arm around it, bringing the box close to my chest. Tilting my head up, I redirect my jets—

The rocks that crashed down hit the lava flow. Molten rock doesn't splash like water, but the impact roils a heat wave my way. My jets slip—

Worst-case scenario.

Regular jets can't handle being this close to lava, and while *my* jets are better, they're not perfect. Everything fails sometimes. I have the box, but it'll mean nothing if I can't get out of this hellish canyon. What should be a simple grab-and-go mission would turn into hours of excruciating climb if my jets fail now . . .

Perfect, I think.

I kick the controls, hard, slamming higher to avoid the lava, my left side bouncing off one part of the still-undulating cliff face. The cry of pain that escapes my lips is real, black smearing my arm even though I don't break my tense grip. The seismic activity is fading already, but my direction's off, a blur in my helmet as my jets sputter. Alarms blare—I'm losing altitude, the temp's rising, the stabilizer's offline. I keep my left arm curled around the box, the hard edges pressing into my suit, as my right hand flails, my boots skidding off the obsidian rock, black flakes falling down before being swallowed by bloody red.

My left boot hits a sharp angle, and my foot wedges inside a crevice at the same time that my hand grabs a rock that doesn't crumble in my grip. More alarms flash over my visor; my vital alerts. Elevated heart rate, adrenaline spike, overheating.

"Ada." I hate how Rian's voice drifts so softly, a question, full of fear. He's not sure I'm still alive.

"Here," I gasp.

"Holy fuck," he says.

"I know."

"Can you—"

"I got it," I say.

"You—I don't care about the box, Ada, you almost died!"

"But I didn't," I say. "And I also got it."

There's some cursing. A lot. It's kind of impressive. He's been taking lessons from Magnusson.

"Okay, okay," Rian says, regaining composure. "You have the box. Can you get back up?" Slight emphasis on *you*, even though I know he means *you with the box*, no matter what he said before.

I tentatively check my position. I'm stable, about fifteen meters above the lava flow, more than triple that away from the nose of the ship. I shot off at an angle when I ricocheted in panic; I'm farther away from both the *Roundabout* and the shuttle we took to get here.

"Jetpack's offline and unstable," I report. I can hear him take a breath, but I interrupt. "I don't have time for whatever you're going to say."

Exhale. "What can I do?"

I press my body against the rock wall, but then test my right foot against a nearby ledge. It doesn't give. I let more weight shift, and even if my legs are spread wider than is comfortable, I feel pretty firm.

"I'm going to have to climb up, and I need both my hands." While I talk, I work on the box. It's a thermal protection unit, but Rian said the contents were small. I break off the first layer and let it drop below, carefully peeling up the top.

Nestled inside the box, under sheets of thincraft wrap, is a cryptex drive.

"Sure hope whatever's on this unit is worth all the trouble," I mutter.

"It is," Rian says gravely. His voice is tense. I like to think it's because he's worried I'm about to die, but maybe it's because I've taken this little drive out of its safe house. "Ada, it . . ." He stops talking, and I stop moving, the weight of what's unsaid making me freeze. "Ada, that device? It's going to help *billions* of people. It's going to help Earth."

He hesitated when he said "Earth," a slight sibilant hiss before he veered away from adding in "Sol" before the word. He's not from Earth—I swear he's got a Rigel-Earth smirk behind those lips—but he knows I am. He knows that I know what Earth is like now, how much it needs help. How much the people need help. He knows that I'm a looter, and by now, he's surely got a strong hypothesis that I'm not the most ethically inclined person, and now he's hoping that I care enough about my homeworld to focus all my ill-gotten skills on getting myself and the drive out of this canyon.

Some people think we should just let Earth die. It's run its course, and the damages of pollution, climate change, and corruption cannot be undone; that's what some people say. They don't care about how it's not exactly easy to just relocate billions of people, how the answer isn't to let an entire world of people die just because others think the place they call home isn't worth the effort to try to save it.

I guess it's a good thing for Rian I'm not one of those people.

"Got it," I say. "Don't die. Or, if I do, toss the drive up first."

"No, just don't die," Rian says, exasperated. Then: "... but yeah, if you've got good aim, chuck it up before you flail down."

"Sarcasm is so sexy."

"I wasn't being sarcastic," he deadpans. "Also, you think I'm sexy?"

"No, I think sarcasm is sexy. You know what else it is?"

"No."

"Distracting."

"Oh." A hiss of static on the comm. "Sorry."

"Just shut up, Sexy." I allow myself a brief moment of triumph when I hear the soft intake of his breath catch as he forces himself not to respond and further keep me from the task at hand.

Keeping as much of my body leaned against the rock

wall as possible, I unzip my front outer pocket and slide the cryptex drive inside. It takes some wiggling to get the tiny thing gripped in my gloves to go in the way I need it to be, but as soon as it's secure, I close the zipper and grab the wall with both hands.

Tilting my head back, my helmet lets me know I've got about sixty-five meters of vertical climbing to get out of this hellhole.

Which is *a lot.*

"What are the chances you can toss down a rope?" I ask.

"We have security cable we can send down," Rian says. "It's the thermal flux that's the problem, though."

The integrity of the line is thrown off by the way the radiant heat from the lava exudes straight up. There's nowhere else for the heat to go, after all.

"I'm tossing down the security line," Rian calls. A moment later, I see a long, insulated cable with a claw clip dropped almost within reach. It shifts. I look up—on the ridge, I can see three people looking down at me. This endeavor's brought Rian out of the ship, at least, and got the others to check out the show.

"But I can't trust this," I say grabbing for the claw and securing it at the loop harness built into my suit.

"Maybe?" Rian's voice cracks. This line is a Hail Mary for if I slip; they can't risk pulling me up with it.

"Climbing up is going to take a long time," I mutter,

scoping out the slick, ridged striations of the oddly formed black rock face.

"What happened to that one goal, full speed stuff?" Rian says. I can tell he's trying to add levity to the situation, but it doesn't help that much. I've still got to climb straight up a wall without falling into a river of molten rock, which isn't exactly something I enjoy doing.

Plus it's hot as fuck.

My hands slip inside my gloves.

I take a deep breath.

New goal. Survive.

Full speed until I do.

It's just that "full speed" is a lot slower right now.

I look up, find a handhold, reach. Push with one foot, find a ledge to step with the other. Up. The line makes this a little easier. I know it's just a single two-centimeter-thick cable between me and plummeting down, but two centimeters are better than nothing.

I check the read outs on my visor. The outer temperature is above what my suit's sensors can measure, which means I'm deeply at risk for damaging my suit. But everything's holding . . . for now.

```
Outer temperature: [WARNING]
Inner temperature: Stable
External download: 2%
Stabilizers: Neutral
```

Air gauge: 82%
Jetpack: Standby

"Hey, Rian?" I ask, reaching for another hold.

"Yeah?" He responds immediately, as if he's been biting back everything he wants to say.

"I've got a long climb ahead. Talk to me?"

11

"Are you asking me for a casual conversation as you climb out of a pit of death?" Rian asks.

"A little light banter couldn't hurt the situation." I have to scoot to reach another handhold. The security line does make me feel safer, as if I might be able to fall and not die, which is better than a hundred percent certainty the opposite direction.

"How's the, er, weather down there?"

"Hot." I swing out, my foot sliding until it catches the ledge I spotted. "Come on; you can do better than that."

"Is distraction a really good idea right now, Ada?"

Okay, I'll be honest. The warmth when he says my name? *That* is what's actually distracting. Probably because he has no idea.

"Bold of you to assume you have anything witty enough to say to actually distract me," I mumble, looking for the next handhold.

"If you're going to insult me, I can just turn off this channel—"

"No!" I say a little too abruptly. I clear my throat. "No. Just . . . I don't know. Tell me about yourself."

"I feel like this is all a giant conspiracy to find out my darkest secrets. Did your jetpack really fail?" He's teasing, but I don't like the implication.

I have to push off a bit to grapple with my next step. It knocks the wind of out me when I slip, scramble, slip, grab.

"Ada?"

"Everything's fine," I say. "So, tell me about your childhood."

Rian barks in laughter. "I'd rather swap places with you."

"I can tell you about my childhood," I offer. "But, you know, it was fairly typical. Boring."

"Really?"

"You sound surprised."

I pause, catching my breath. I'm feeling the weight of my jetpack and life-support unit right now. This shit's *heavy* when you're clutching toeholds on a sheer cliff face. And unlike in space, this damn planet has gravity.

At least the temperature lowers the higher I climb. It's still too hot outside for my suit to register a number, but the warning has reduced from neon orange to neon yellow, so that's nice.

"What are the others doing?" I ask. "Because this is kind of a shitty job, not going to lie, and it would make me feel better if you told me Magnusson was rooting through cycler worms to try to find the next item you need."

I scan the other data I'm tracking in my visor screen. Download at thirty-two percent; jetpacks on standby. Looks like I'm going to keep doing this the hard way.

"Yadav is checking seismic activity," Rian says. "But what makes you think Magnusson is looking for another item?" He's teasing. He knows I know the real mission he's on is twofold. He's been letting things slip intentionally for a while now.

"I'm hanging off the side of a cliff with something so valuable, you crossed the galaxy at top speed to get here for it," I say. "Don't play coy. Plus, I opened the box, remember? I know this thing you want is a cryptex drive."

I get up another little ridge. My shoulders are screaming. I've been in space too long for this shit.

"So," I continue, panting, "you're going to all this trouble to get a cryptex drive. But thing about those kinds of drives? They require a key. A physical key. And I'm just really hoping that you're making Magnusson sort through the sewage pit of that ship to see if it's there."

I examine my choices. The higher I go, the fewer options I'm seeing to climb out. I test the safety line Rian dropped me; it's taut, and it seems secure. At least the higher I go, the less chance I have of the external heat making this snap right when I really need it.

Rian chuckles. "What makes you think that we need a key for the cryptex drive?"

"Other than the fact that it's a cryptex? Come on; I know my tech. That sort of drive is full of encoded data that cannot be translated without a key." I've seen the sort before. They're pricey, but if you want to secure your information, that's the best way. A cryptex drive's contents can still be downloaded anywhere—no data is secure these days, anyway, and if there's a strong-enough uplink, anyone can get information. A cryptex key, though? That's offline. Can't be downloaded. You can only get the encryption code if you have the physical digits in your hand.

The box I'm carrying right now has the information Rian or whatever office he works for wants. But it's useless and impossible to get any of that information if they cannot locate the key.

"No, you're right," Rian says, "of course I need a key for the cryptex drive. I meant, what makes you think we don't already have it?"

I chuckle. "Because you've sent Magnusson searching in the trash compactor for it."

"No, I haven't," Rian says. There's a long pause, long enough for me to wrench myself up another meter or so. "But yes, he's looking for the key."

"You're having him search the wrong spot," I say.

"Because you want him to search in the hardest-to-reach

areas that also are the dirtiest and most disgusting? I don't think the crew of the *Roundabout* chucked the key in the trash, Ada."

"No, but the cryptex drive was on the bridge, in a secure location, yeah? I saw the bridge—the lockbox broke in the crash, and the fact that this drive is here makes it likely that it was ejected from there." There's a particularly wide outcrop of rock above me and to the left, big enough for me to take a breather. I hoist myself up, my leg slipping twice before I can make it. Once I'm on the rock, I crawl on my hands and knees until I'm at the widest area, then carefully twist around so I don't mess up my jetpack or life-support unit. There's just enough seat left over for me to dangle my legs over the edge, the lava river glowing beneath me.

"So, if I were the one ensuring super important data was kept safe," I continue once I catch my breath, "I'd put the drive in one part of the ship and the key in the other."

"Are you suggesting the key's in the cargo hold?"

"I'm just saying that's where I'd put it. Not that they thought their ship was going to crash and break in two. Just—if it's top-secret information, it makes sense to put the key that can open the lock in the furthest place possible from it. And short of cramming the key up the exhaust, the cargo hold makes sense."

I can almost hear the gears in Rian's head churning. The cryptex drive was protected on the bridge, arguably the most secure location on the ship. Despite its size, the *Roundabout* could be manned by a minimal crew, maybe eight or a dozen members, tops. It wasn't like it was a cruiser with hundreds of people on board, all of them nosy or bumbling around into areas they shouldn't go to.

"If you want to protect something," I say, resting my head back on the cliff face, "there are two ways to do it. First, make it obvious. Put the cryptex drive in a highly secure location and make sure everyone knows it's off limits and guarded."

"Second, toss the key in the cargo hold."

"I saw the remains of that part of the ship. There were nearly a hundred transport crates. A cryptex key is no bigger than my finger, yeah? So, just pack it away in a box. Make it a needle in the haystack. And don't even tell anyone that's where you hid it, so they don't even know to look there."

I can tell Rian's with me on this. After a while, he says, "You good, Lamarr?"

"I've found a nice spot to sit and contemplate all the bad life choices that brought me to a river of lava I have to climb out of."

"Okay. Sit tight for a bit; let me send Magnusson over to the aft part of the ship."

"I've got all the time in the world."

I swing my legs, thinking. I wonder what Magnusson is going to find in the cargo hold. I check my readouts. My suit's finally not screaming about the external temp—the warning is now green and flashing *inadvisable conditions* rather than polite tech speech for *certain death*, so that's good.

"Lamarr?" Rian's voice fills my ear again.

"I wish you'd just call me Ada."

"Ada."

I can't explain it, but I swear his voice grows softer when he uses my given name. It's almost enough to make a girl swoon, if she weren't sitting on a little ledge on the side of a cliff.

"I suppose I should start climbing again." My voice is resigned.

"Are your jetpacks still not functioning?" Rian asks.

```
External download: 78%
Stabilizers: Neutral
Air gauge: 64%
Jetpack: Standby
```

"Nope, they're offline," I say. "I think when I finally get back up, you need to tell Captain Ursula that I deserve quadruple portions of the meal today."

"You can eat everything in the supplies that you want," Rian laughs. "Plus, there's a special meal for tonight."

"Special? Hell, you should have started with that. Is there going to be cheese? Because I'd scale a cliff for cheese."

"I'm not sure, actually. I just know we have some celebratory—"

"How can you not be sure about *cheese*?!"

Rian laughs, as if this were a laughing matter. "I promise it'll be worth the effort."

"I'm going to need that in writing."

"You have my word."

I sigh. Time to get moving again. Before I can talk my jelly legs into working, I use my sight-line tracker to estimate the distance I have left until I reach the top. At the rate I'm going, another hour or two at least.

I force my body up. "Do you think First will give me a massage when I get back on the *Halifax*?"

"Maybe. But there's also a dry-heat pulser, if you want."

I whistle. Damn, the *Halifax* is a nice ship. "Remind me to scavenge that when you guys crash."

Rian laughs. "Crashing's not in the plans."

"Okay, but *if* it does, I'm calling looter's rights now."

"Noted."

There's some crackly silence as I heft up, starting the climb up the wall again. I'm slower now, the strain of the day wearing on me.

I'm so close, I think. *Not much longer . . .*

"Tell me about your worst job." Rian's voice almost comes as a surprise, and it spurs me on to find another grab, pull my body up a little more, keep going.

"Worst job?" I snort. "You mean other than this?"

"Other than this." He pauses. "Or something. I just thought it may help take your mind off . . . all of this."

"Yeah, okay," I say. "It's an easy question, anyway." I don't answer as I climb a little farther up. I miss my ledge. It wasn't the comfiest spot I've ever sat on, but I liked not moving for a while. Not-moving is a pastime of mine I'm particularly fond of.

"So, this was maybe two years ago," I say. "Got word of a ghost ship. Easy pickings, out in the middle of nowhere. I think the people on board were trying to relocate or something; I don't know."

I said it was an easy question, but the answer isn't easy. Rian lets silence stretch as I focus on the climb, my mind back on the ghost ship.

I don't want to think about this. I *hate* this memory. But recounting it between climbs, filling my long breaks with words . . . it was Rian's idea, but it's a good one.

A distraction is *exactly* what I need right now.

My eyes sting, my vision blurs. Which sucks, because it's not like I can take my helmet off and wipe my face. I let out a deep breath. I should have lied about the whole damn thing, made up a story, not let myself remember this.

But that's the thing about tragedy.

It's hard to lie about.

12

Two Years Ago

Most ships don't crash like the *Roundabout* did. They don't hit planets. Most ships that are lost are lost at either takeoff or landing. That's the dangerous bit. Leaving a world or coming home to one. The stuff in the middle? That's the easy part. Coasting through the black. Little to hit, few reasons to break out the highly volatile fuel.

But I wouldn't have a job if things never went wrong.

If a ship malfunctions in flight, typically there's a warning. Escape pods go out, the crew's picked up, and if it's not worth hauling back anywhere, they let the dead ship float, empty. Perfect for looting.

The other kind of ghost ship is the kind where the escape pods don't go out.

I've seen it more than once. Sometimes sabotage, particularly if it's a competing company. Sometimes attack. There are pirates. Some tiny worlds with cult-like colonies that fiercely protect their sector. No one ever said space was safe, and then humans go in and make it even less so.

I once came across a ghost ship that broadcast a perpetual

biohazard warning on loop. I brought *Glory* close, using the front flood lamp to illuminate the dark windows. There weren't many portholes that could show me anything, but I'll never forget the way the bridge looked. A beam of light cutting across the grotesquely twisted faces. Some sort of sickness; I don't know what. Killed them all. Half a dozen people, at least, all piled up in the nose of the ship, fingers splayed on the carbonglass as if they'd been trying to scratch their way to the void. *Glory*'s light made their open eyes reflect strangely. It felt like they were watching me. I didn't board that ship.

The *Rose* was something else.

I did all the scans. Checked everything. I could tell before I boarded that the ship had had a major malfunction, the escape pods hadn't been evacuated, and there was no one left alive on board. Floating in space with a full cargo meant it was an easy job. I opened up *Glory*'s bay door, flew out to the *Rose*. This was before I had a jaxon jet, just a regular unit.

To get in, I had to activate the emergency latch on the depressurization chamber, but the ship was completely dead—no power at all, let alone gravity generators, oxygen flow, or any other type of life support. There was nothing to stop me from cranking open the door; it was designed to be accessed in case of a breach or failure like this.

I can never explain the full eeriness of a ghost ship. Even the ones where I know what's happened, boarding a ghost is like a violation. You're going into someone's home. You should be stopped.

Because every ship is a home. People like Captain Ursula, who treats the *Halifax* like a tool, don't always know that. But I bet Nandina sees the med bay as her home, even if this is a temporary job for her, even if she claims otherwise. Humans do that. They turn the place where they feel safe into a home, and even when they know that home won't last, they fall in love with it. A little, anyway.

Ghost ships are dark. Fuck, *space* is dark. People forget that because we use external floodlights and internal electronics, and when a ship is lived in, it's never fully dark. But ghost ships are.

When I boarded the *Rose,* I had my helmet's headlamp on, and I had two handhelds in my belt. I always carry extra lights on ghost-ship salvages; I learned the hard way how difficult it is to get off a ship that's not yours when your light goes dark.

But the glow from headlamps and handhelds is dim, sporadic. They illuminate a circle at a time, and they cast shadows, long shadows that shouldn't exist in space.

Not everything wants to be seen.

It wasn't the bodies that bothered me on the *Rose.* To be honest, I expected the bodies. No pods evacuated, no shuttle . . . a ship doesn't fly without a crew. So, a dead ship would have dead humans on board. That was always going to be the case.

What got me was that it had been a family. Eight people total. One elderly man, three middle-aged adults, four children. I found them in various parts of the ship. The older man and one adult were on the bridge. I found another adult in the mess hall. The third adult, a female with long black hair that hid her face, floating around her like a halo, was in a room with all the children. There were little toys—building blocks and a stuffed animal and those posable dolls that can interact with augmented reality games but are still fun on their own.

None of them were strapped down, not even the people on the bridge. They were all floating. Which meant that they didn't actively crash—they were just living their lives. Until something went wrong. Something sudden. Something catastrophic.

I had to find out. I located the record box in the bridge, the thing every ship is required to have, took it back to *Glory*, and hooked it up to power. *Something* evacuated all the oxygen on the ship. There was a record of a slow leak for a long time—at least two cycles—but the life-support unit compensated, so there was no noticeable decrease in available air. Then something broke, and all the O_2 was discharged at once.

None of this felt like sabotage, but it also didn't make sense.

I dug deeper.

Some repairs—to fix the leak, I assume—had been made to the O$_2$ filter. I went back aboard the *Rose*, careful this time to avoid seeing the bodies. Took the main panel down, removed the unit. I didn't notice it at first. I had to use my visor's visual enhancements to see the tiny crack in the O-ring. A little circle used to seal the outtake tube. It was small enough to slide over my gloved finger, although that made the hairline break in the plexi-steel more visible.

I spent hours in the dark, trying to see if there was anything else.

But in the end, it came down to one O-ring. One individual part. Those damn things cost almost nothing on land. You can pick them up at any dock.

They're so tiny.

But when the seal broke, the tube popped off.

There were supposed to be failsafes; of course there were. Every ship has automatic failsafes.

But this had been quick.

And the failsafes had failed.

And the entire ship had died because one tiny ring cracked.

I've been telling this story to Rian the whole time I'm making my slow way back up the cliff.

But what I don't tell him is this:

That moment changed me on a core level. I can see that cracked O-ring as clearly as I can see the world in front of me. I wake up every morning, and I remind myself how futile it all is. You can do everything right, try to be good, try to do good, and sometimes it won't matter. Your O-ring gets a crack in it, and you die before you have time to panic. A nothing part, ignored until it's broken, and then you're dead.

You and everyone you love just cease to be.

That's how close life and death are. Not just here, in space or on a volatile planet. Everywhere. Everywhere in the universe, you're one cracked O-ring away from total failure. And we all just go through each day, ignoring that.

Pretending like we don't see the cracks.

Like the cracks aren't going to break all the way.

Life is a fucking miracle. How did the right atoms collide and the right DNA strands evolve and the right lucky breaks in planetary development build up over trillions of years in the impossible expanse of all of time and space to make *you*? A series of accidents and luck and planning and fate and maybe God or maybe just the sheer chaos of it all conspired to make the life within you, all eternity stretching to a pinpoint that coincides with your first breath.

And a tiny cracked O-ring can take it all away.

It's so, *so* hard to live.

And so, *so* easy to die.

It's just that the O-ring is deep inside the life-support unit, buried under outtake valves and wiring harnesses and bypass tubes. You have to look for it.

You have to look for the crack in it.

But you can't forget it's there. You can't ever forget that.

Telling this has taken more time than I anticipated. But it's served Rian's goal well; I forgot about the physical pain of climbing. I was back on the *Rose*, back in the dark, not here, scaling a cliff.

I can see the top of the ridge now, can see Rian's helmeted face peering over the edge at me. Almost there.

I track my course—not much farther—but pull in close on a ledge that is big enough for me to stand with both feet planted. I keep my front to the wall.

"What are you doing?" Rian asks.

"Just one quick break before the end," I say. "I'm not my best right now." One wrong move, and all this work will be for nothing.

I check my visor's readouts. *Fucking finally*, I think fiercely. A few adjustments to my suit, and I'm exactly where I want to be.

"All right, I told you my worst day," I say, starting to climb again. "Tell me yours."

"Oh, that's too long of a story." Rian sounds happier now. "You're almost out."

I heave myself up to another handhold, scrambling my legs until I get traction. At least my boots grip well. I feel the line tighten—Rian's risking the manual crank to help me, reaching down toward me with one gloved hand.

"Fine, tell me about your best day, then," I say.

"That's easy." He's close enough now that I can see his grinning face behind his visor. "Today. Today's the best day."

My hand reaches his, and he yanks me up the last bit. I fall down on the flat rock at the top of the cliff, panting, staring up at the stars and the void between them.

My hand still in his.

13

I unzip my outer pouch and pass over the cryptex drive to Rian. "Comm Magnusson," I tell him. "First isn't down here, and I need him."

"Need him? Why?" Rian asks.

"To carry me."

"You say that like you don't scale cliffs in your spare time on a regular basis." Rian's joking with me, but I notice that he's pretty damn careful about storing the cryptex drive in his suit's pocket. He ignores me as I stare up at the black sky and millions of stars and wonder when my muscles will quit burning.

I'm lying flat on my back, but I hold my arms up. "You'll do if Magnusson is busy."

"I'm not carrying you, Ada."

Oof, I do like the way that man says my name. Leave it to me to develop a crush on the enemy.

Rian bends down when I don't move even after he summons Saraswati and Magnusson to meet back on the shuttle. *Now* concern's written all over his face under his helmet. "Are you okay? That was a big climb, and—"

"Ugh, you ruin it when you treat me like that," I say, scrambling up. "I'm fine; let's go back to the ship and get something to eat. And by *something*, I mean *everything*."

I hear a snort of appreciation from him as he sets his pace to match my own slower one.

In the distance, Magnusson approaches the shuttle from one direction—where the aft wreckage is—and Saraswati is several paces ahead of us.

"Switch over to the public comm channel," Rian tells me. As soon as I do, I hear Magnusson reporting in—he found nothing but debris.

"Incoming," Saraswati says, interrupting him. Her voice is pitched high. "We're getting at least two soon. Volcanic eruption four klicks north indicates a plate shift—"

Before she finishes speaking, the earth undulates. Rian grabs my arm, holding me up. "Can you run?" he asks, already half-dragging me into a quicker pace.

I don't want to, but I also don't want to let this planet eat me, so I start jogging, my legs burning. In the distance I see a bright spurt of orange-red—the volcano Saraswati was keeping an eye on has erupted. Moments later, the earth rumbles. We're almost to the ship. Rian's about to rip my arm off, he's yanking me so hard, but I don't mind. The only thing that's in our favor is that the land here is pretty flat and hard, but the only reason the land here is flat and hard is because it's dried-up lava, and that sort of indicates we're right in the middle of where the flow is going to reach.

Magnusson and Saraswati are already inside the shuttle when Rian and I race up the ramp. I stumble the last few steps—Magnusson started raising the ramp before I was completely off it—and Rian catches me. The shuttle lurches as Magnusson takes off, sending both me and Rian crashing onto the floor.

"Not exactly how I pictured you under me," I mutter.

"What?" Rian asks.

"Nothing." I push up, staggering as the shuttle shifts again. "We need to get strapped in."

We make our rocky way up to the command center of the shuttle. Magnusson is focused on the controls, but Saraswati turns as Rian and I grab our seats and hastily harness in.

"All good?" she asks, already turning back to the controls before we answer.

"We'll live," Rian says. His brow furrows when he looks at me, though. My suit's messy, but overall, everything's working inside and out. I think. I'll do a recharge and full diagnostic back on the *Halifax*.

I turn my attention to the main carbonglass window extending over the nose. The flat, black land Rian and I were just running over is starting to crack, snaking lines of bright lava infiltrating the desolate landscape.

"Oh, shit," Magnusson whispers under his breath as the

rift I just climbed out of shivers, the edges rippling. It's beautiful, but it's also horrific, witnessing the way a world is born, how easy it all falls apart. It will be formed again and again, the surface of this planet, and one day it will be whole and stable and perhaps even full of life. But it must break first. Again. And again.

On the ground below, the forward section of the *Roundabout*, including the bridge that held the cryptex drive, jostles free from the tentative position it held, crashing down into the rift. The rift itself grinds like the maw of a hungry monster, shifting and crunching as lava sprays up. It's enough of a heat blast to blow the shuttle back before Magnusson gets it restabilized.

"That was good timing," I say. "I mean, if that thing was going to drop into the lava, at least it waited until I had the cryptex drive first. And until I was out of the rift."

Saraswati twists around in her seat again, straining against the harness just to give me an incredulous look. Sure, if I'd been an hour later in climbing out of the rift, I'd be dead, but that was the point of me saying it was good timing. Any timing that doesn't end in death by lava is good timing. Obviously.

"Let's get the hell out of here," Rian says. He grips the grab bar by his seat, and even if his hands are gloved, I suspect his knuckles are white.

Magnusson tilts the nose of the shuttle up, the horizon dipping down.

"Are all your missions this exciting?" I ask as the thrusters slam us back into our seats. "I would definitely prefer a little heads-up next time. Also, remind me to negotiate hazard pay with my buddy Ursula."

One of them snorts, but I can't tell over the comm who it was.

Everyone's there to greet us in the shuttle bay by the time the area's repressurized. The captain stands in front, but Nandina and First are at attention, tense. I'm the last one off the shuttle, and while Ursula already has Rian distracted and reporting in on the success of retrieving the cryptex drive, Nandina rushes to me.

"Your suit's not connected to our system, so I couldn't monitor you, but Rian let us know that you sustained multiple impact injuries in a jetpack malfunction and then rigorous activity when you—"

"I'm fine," I say, dismissing her.

She does a once-over on my suit, coated in black dust.

"It was interesting down there," I allow. Then I turn my attention to First. "Would have been easier if you'd been there to carry me. I had to *walk* back to the shuttle. And then also *run*."

"My apologies," First says with an expressionless face.

My whole body aches, but there's not that much I can do about it until I can get this suit off and get cleaned up. Magnusson and Saraswati are already heading up to the main part of the ship, so I trudge up after them.

Just before I go through the door, I hear the captain gasp. *"Really?"* she says in a carrying voice. When I glance over, both she and Rian are watching me.

I know what they're thinking. I'm not a member of their elite crew, and I got the cryptex drive. And, even more surprisingly, I just handed it over to them. I don't look back again. I don't want or need the drive in Rian's hand. It's locked, and they can't access any of the information on it unless they find the cryptex key, and they have no idea where that is. And now that the forward part of the ship fell into a river of lava, there's only one place left for them to search—through every single cargo crate and piece of debris scattered over the volatile earth from the aft section.

In my bunk, I carefully peel away my suit. The moisture-wicking inner liner smells rank; I've pushed that to the limit for sure. Before I do anything else, I hoist my life-support unit and jetpack up to the rechargers, then do a thorough inspection of the suit itself.

My body is sore from the climb, but there's a different sort of tension winding in my shoulders now.

Everything's falling into place.

After making sure my suit is exactly the way I need it to be,

I slide into the tiny wash unit connected to my room. My body goes through the motions—scrub sponge with antiseptic, vita lotion into my sore muscles, clean comb through my hair.

Elsewhere on the ship, Magnusson and Saraswati are probably doing the same things I am. And Rian would need to get out of his suit too, get cleaned up. I think he'd trust Ursula with the cryptex drive. He must. Yes, he had to have given it to her, and she has some secure location on the ship to store it. The bridge, perhaps, just like the *Roundabout* had done. That standard lockbox. Ursula and First will take turns guarding that drive. They might not have if I weren't here, but . . . they might.

I wonder if Saraswati or Magnusson or Nandina know what information is on that drive.

I wonder if the captain or First do.

I know Rian does.

I saw the way he took it from me, the way he looked when he held it.

He knows not only what it is but why it is so important. Beyond what he told me.

He knows.

All I have to do is make him think that I don't.

14

Sure enough, the captain's not in the mess hall when it's time to eat. Guard duty, I guarantee it. I didn't check, though. Didn't wander around, look for where a new lock's been set. I went straight from a fresh set of clothing to food.

All the others, except for Ursula, are there. Magnusson stands by the dispenser with a covered box on his tray.

"Who would have thought you'd be the last one to eat?" Magnusson says, but he's grinning, even as I take the tray from him and make him get a new one.

My heart's racing as I sit down. I think Saraswati says something, but I don't hear it. See, on a deep-space ship, the food's mostly dried goods that pretend to be edible, and even the good stuff on a ship isn't the *real* stuff, you know? But food that comes in a box? Food that comes in a box like this is special. There's not much room for frozen goods. But frozen food is often . . .

"*Ohhh.*" A decadent groan escapes my lips, and Rian chuckles.

Beneath the foil-lined top on the box is a real piece of meat. Like, real *real*. Not a composite. Not replacement protein patties. *Real* meat.

"Chicken breast, green beans, mashed potatoes," Nandina says proudly.

Potatoes. I thought the meat was something, but potatoes? I haven't had actual potatoes since I left Earth.

"Wait for it," Rian says, reaching over the table to point to the little foil wrapped block on the side.

"No," I say, my voice rising, sounding almost angry.

"Yes."

"No." My hand shakes as I pick up the cube. It's cold but a little soft. I carefully pull back the foil.

Butter.

There are actual tears in my eyes as I look around the room. Their bemused smiles are proof enough that this is a meal they all knew was coming, a celebration for finding part of what they'd come all this way to find.

"I'm never leaving this crew," I say. "You don't even have to pay me. Just feed me."

Magnusson puts his new tray down beside mine. "Hear, hear."

I grab a fork and stab the chicken, lifting the whole breast up and cramming as much as I can into my mouth. "You can use a knife," Rian laughs, but he's wrong. The thing about real meat that I miss so, so much is the feel of it in my teeth. The way my mouth has to work for the prize. The way it's not uniform.

This chicken has never been in a tube, and I know that with every sense in my body.

It hurts to swallow; it's too much, and it's not liquid; it doesn't slide. I don't care. The pain is part of the pleasure.

Across from me, Rian calmly cuts a piece of his chicken with a knife. I'm ripping apart my second bite before he even lifts his fork to his lips. Magnusson is mashing the butter into his potatoes like it's a sacred rite. I can respect that. On my other side, First is experimenting—dipping the chicken in the mashed potatoes, then stabbing some green beans and stuffing them in their mouth before they swallow. Saraswati's started with the green beans. Bad choice. They're the weak link here; a vegetable and too soft and too close to standard fare. Maybe she's saving the best for last. I don't understand that mindset. Nandina's like me, meat first, attacked with the brutality such a rare treat deserves. I knew I liked her the best.

I shear another piece of chicken off with my teeth, and Rian shakes his head. "If you eat too quickly, it'll just be gone. Savor it."

"You said I get three servings," I say around a mouthful.

"Well, there are only five boxes," Rian says. "So, you can have more food, but it won't be this."

I chew slower.

The captain's not here. Guarding the cryptex drive, surely. But also giving me her celebratory dinner. I guess that makes up for leaving me to die with only one percent air in my tank.

"What's the meal going to be when we find the key to the drive?" I ask.

"Steak," Rian says. "And ice cream."

"Fuck," I breathe, barely audible.

Nandina puts down her fork. She didn't know how much I knew about the ship's mission, only that I already knew that there was a second piece needed to succeed. She knows now. When she starts eating again, I think, *That's all of them. They accept me now.* Even the captain—when she found out I was the one who retrieved the drive, I could see a glimmer of respect in her shocked eyes. They've seen what I can do, and while I'm still a wild card in this carefully planned salvage mission, they trust me.

They . . . trust me.

They shouldn't. But they do.

I swallow dryly.

It's a bittersweet revelation.

I don't like it.

But I also kind of do.

I'm not used to this, trust. The easiness of sitting at a table and sharing a meal and feeling like there's nothing to hide. It's . . . weird.

"You know," First says, "you could be a part of the regular crew, if you wanted. Captain said so."

I shoot a glance at Rian. "Told you she loves me."

He cocks an eyebrow. "*Love* is a strong word."

I ignore that and turn back to First. "I suppose climbing up the rift was my interview?"

"At least you didn't have to supply five different references and a background check," Saraswati mutters.

Background check. They've probably already run one on me. Not something too intense—communication is still slow, but the *Halifax* might have a data linkup that could ping off the portals for some quick info, the basics. I dip my fork into my mashed potatoes, swirling the melted yellow into the creamy white. When I look up at Rian, he's watching me intently. *Definitely* did a background check.

"I can't join this crew," I say, eyes sliding from his. "I'd be bored to death. But I'll hitch a ride to civilization."

"Well, we have you for a few weeks at least, then, anyway," Rian says softly.

Something biting and sarcastic is just waiting to fall out of my mouth, but then . . . nothing.

He lifts his water bottle in the air. "To Ada."

The others pause their meal, also lifting their glass.

Oh, no.

Oh, I hate this.

"The bravest of us all," Magnusson adds.

"Or the stupidest," Saraswati says. "There's no way in hell I'd have gone down there, even with your jetpack, Ada."

"It's a good jetpack," I say.

"Not good enough," Magnusson says. "It got you down there but not back up."

I swallow the automatic response rising in my throat. I'm proud of my suit, proud of its mods, most of which I've done myself. I force my shoulders down and say, "It all worked out."

Saraswati nods. "The rest of this is going to be tedious but not nearly as dangerous. Most of the debris field is relatively stable, far enough away from the existing fault line that I don't think we're going to have any more dramatic quakes that directly impact our search."

"That's too bad." I fake a groan, and the others all laugh, and the conversation swings around to regular chatter.

After the boxes are empty, I take my tray back to the dispenser and get some of the regular food. Lentils aren't quite as exciting now that I've had meat, but they're still better than what I'd been living off of. As I slurp it down, I let myself pretend.

Pretend that Saraswati and Nandina can be my friends. That First and the captain like me. That Magnusson sees me as an equal, which is about the highest praise I think the man could give.

That Rian . . .

I can pretend.

For just this night.

15

When the meal is done, the others drift off until it's just me and Rian. All the boxes are empty now.

I meet his eyes, and for once, I don't think about the tiny gears working behind them. I let myself drown in their clear, bright hazel.

"What are you thinking about?" Rian asks, his brow furrowing, disrupting my view.

"Just wondering how secure the freezer unit is, and if I can break into it with the tools I have, and if—no, *when*, I do, whether or not Magnusson will evac me through the hatch after I eat all the portions of ice cream."

"Very secure, probably you can, and absolutely he will," Rian says smoothly, standing. "Come with me."

"No." I settle my butt in the hard seat. "You promised me more food."

"Come with me," he repeats, a smile cracking his impatient look. "I have something better than what's in the dispenser."

I stand, and Rian leads me toward the corridor with the

bunks. "Please don't take this as an insult," I say, "but if you intend to show me your bedroom and expect me to want . . ." I gesture at his body. ". . . more than ice cream, you are mistaken."

"You said I was sexy," Rian states flatly.

"Ice cream is sexier."

Rian presses a button, and a door zips open, revealing a standard-issue bunk room similar to the one I was given. Larger, though. Two windows.

I step inside, Rian following. "I don't have ice cream."

I turn on my heel, heading out the door. Rian grabs my arm and tugs me back inside, laughing. "But I have something better."

"Statistically impossible," I say, pulling my elbow free and crossing my arms over my chest. "But I'm willing to test your theory."

Rian goes over to a storage drawer. I look around his room. The bed's unmade. I don't know why I find that charming, but I do. Rian's so orderly, every thought lined up inside his head like one of those old-style libraries, neat little categorized volumes of knowledge in a row. But his cover's tossed to one side, a thin blanket twisted up, his pillow dented from where his head lay.

"Here." Rian puts something soft and round and fuzzy in my hand.

I can smell it faintly. There's an earthy scent to it as well as a sweetness. I turn it over in my palm. It's not uniformly round; there's a thin line from where a stem had been all the way to the barest hint of a point at the bottom.

"It's a peach," he says.

"No, it's not. Peaches are slick." I rub my fingers over the light grayish fuzz of this fruit. I think if I pressed hard, I'd break the skin. Part of me wants to.

"And orange in color?" Rian asks.

I nod.

"That's a canned peach," he says. "This is a fresh one."

The tip of my pinky touches the hard spot at the indented top. I've seen pictures of fruit growing on trees; I know this is where the stem connected it to the branch, and the branch connected to a tree, and the tree grew roots into the soil. I've seen hardwoods and pines and spruces when I lived in America; I've seen citrus and olive and cypress in Malta.

I've never seen a peach tree. I've never seen a peach.

Not like this. Fresh.

Real.

"Do I just . . ." I lift the fruit to my mouth.

"Let me peel it first." Rian plucks it from my fingers and turns to the little table between his two windows.

I was absolutely going to quip something smartass at him, but then I see the flash of a silver blade in his hand. With skill born from practice, Rian glides the knife between the fuzzy skin and the smooth, pinkish-red flesh of the peach, the bright inside a startling contrast against the dull outer layer.

"Peaches are orange," I insist despite the evidence to the contrary, but I'm more than half-distracted by the way the fruit juices slick his fingers.

He cuts a slice and passes it to me. The shape is now familiar to me, but there are hard filaments on the inner edge where the stone had been. And the color . . . I twist the slice around, inspecting it.

Rian huffs a little laugh through his nose. "Canned peaches are orange," he says. "This is a red vineyard peach. Try it."

I almost don't want to bite into it; it's too much of a jewel. But when I do, a burst of flavors explodes on my tongue. While dinner tonight had been decadent and rich, this peach is light. It tastes like sunshine and joy. I close my eyes, mashing the fruit against my tongue, relishing not just the taste but the *feel* of it.

"I knew I could get you to savor something," Rian says, his voice deep.

My eyes fly open, and I snatch the rest of the peach out of his hand, eating it so voraciously that juice dribbles down my chin. I suck my sticky fingers clean, and I would have eaten the stone that had been in the center of the peach had Rian not taken it and thrown it into the composter with the peelings. "Trust me," he says, laughing, "you don't want to eat that part."

I hold my hand out. "More."

"That's the only one I have."

I narrow my eyes. I can read him well enough to know he's telling the truth. But I'm still tempted to tear apart his cabin and make sure. Instead, I sit down on the edge of his bed, deeply aware of the blanket, the way his legs probably tangled in it last night.

"My family are farmers on Rigel-Earth," he says, and I can't tell if his tone is rueful or if he's just lost in memories. "That's one of our best-selling crops."

Rigel-Earth, I think. *I fucking knew it.*

Oh, well. No man's perfect.

"You were saving that one, weren't you?" I ask. "The peach. We all get a celebratory dinner, but you were saving that one for yourself."

"I'm sure the others brought items from home with them. We all have an allocated trunk."

Standard operation. But a fruit like that is perishable. Easily bruised and destroyed. This took care. I'd bet coin no one else on the *Halifax* packed something like this.

I should thank him. Instead, I say, "I had no idea Rigel-Earth made peaches like this."

"Sol-Earth did it first," Rian says.

My eyes go up in shock.

"It's from a variety in midwestern Europe," he continues. I keep my face placid; the man just gave me fresh fruit, I'm not going to mock him for not knowing "midwestern Europe" isn't really a thing people say. It's not like Germany is Minnesota. It's a moot point, anyway. Neither of those exist anymore. Minnesota's mostly underwater now, and Germany, like all the countries of Western Europe, is a part of the tourism board, no longer independent and individual nations.

"That's what my family does," Rian adds. "We're heirloom farmers."

See, there's a difference between someone scratching the earth and hoping to feed their family and an heirloom farmer who spends a lot of money to sell produce at an up-charge based on where the seeds came from.

Only Rigel-Earth would come up with the concept of luxury food.

"You're a long way from the field," I say.

"Closer than you think," he says, and now we're both thinking of the cryptex drive and what's on it.

Rian sits down beside me. The mattress dips, gravity pulling us a little closer. He turns to me, searching my eyes. "I didn't mean for you to risk your life for the cryptex drive," he says.

I shrug.

Rian shakes his head. "No. Don't treat it like it was nothing. It wasn't."

Way to make things awkward. I look down at my hands in my lap, my jaw clenching.

Rian takes the hint. His gaze goes to the windows. "My sister's a rover. On Sol-Earth."

"Please don't tell me I remind you of your sister, because that's going to make seducing you later kind of gross," I say.

Rian snorts. Being a rover is like being a looter. The difference is, a rover is a nomad explorer of the unprotected areas of Earth. This peach came from a variety originally found in Europe? There's a pretty big landhopper network in Europe—tours that go down the Rhine valley, that meander through Paris, that cruise along the remains of the dikes in the flooded northwest, windmill sails peeking up over the flat water.

A rover wouldn't see those areas, the ones protected with little pockets of bots and droids to keep the area clean and livable.

A rover goes into the *other* areas, the places where landhoppers cover their windows with vid screens to block tourists' views so they don't witness the way pollution has soiled the homeworld we all share if you go back far enough in all of our ancestry. Rovers risk the radiation sickness and the pollution and the mutated wildlife and everything else to find things to sell.

And nothing sells as well as viable plant life. Gold and diamonds are on every world, and some of the other planets have gemstones even rarer than the ones Earth has. A rock looks like a rock anywhere; some are just shinier than others.

But nothing I've ever tasted before tastes like the peach I just had.

Luxury food.

I've never been rich enough to consider that a possibility. I can barely wrap my head around it.

"I haven't seen her in a long time," Rian says, and it take a moment for my mind to go back to our conversation, to his sister, the rover. From his face, I can guess that maybe she went out on an expedition and didn't come back. I don't want to ask, though. It doesn't feel right to take more than he's giving right now.

But it's a story I know well. Everyone on Earth knows someone who wanted something more, something better than the little bubbles of livable but inescapable life. Some of us, like me and Magnusson, go to space. Some, like Saraswati's parents, emigrate.

But we all know someone who decided to risk it in the unprotected lands. And we all know someone who never came back from that.

"It's not too late," Rian tells me. "I . . . I *can't* tell you more about what this mission is for, but you deserve to know that what you did today was important."

He's dropping clues so heavy, it's like he's begging me to guess the top-secret intel. "I know the drive I rescued is full of some sort of important data," I say, giving him this much. "Now I'm thinking it's linked to fixing up Earth?" I raise my eyebrows at him. Rian betrays no expression, his face perfectly blank—which is the answer I'm seeking.

"Oh," I breathe. "Oh. That *is* clever."

"What is?" he asks.

"It's not just the data that's important. It's the ship's path. *Roundabout,* I mean. It wasn't just going on an out-of-the-way route—it was going to an out-of-the-way planet. And it's not just data, is it?" I jump up and start pacing the room. Rian watches me as I take three strides, turn, take three more. I stop abruptly, staring at Rian and tapping my chin, considering.

He keeps the poker face, but his eyes are sparkling in anticipation.

"The *Roundabout*'s path was going to take it to a world without atmosphere, one of the remote planets," I continue, watching his face carefully for a flicker of acknowledgement that I'm right. "If this mission is linked to nature . . . you're testing something that will clean up the pollution or purify the air or something like that for Earth, and you tried to send the drive to a manufacturing world that has no atmo so it could be tested . . ." I muse out loud, taking up the puzzle pieces Rian's giving me and sifting them into the picture he wants me to see, the one he thinks I didn't know about already.

"The other thing you're looking for, the other piece, it's not *just* the key to the cryptex drive. It's . . ." He doesn't flinch, so I have to pretend to guess. "A climate-cleaner of some sort. A prototype. Maybe a chemical combination or some sort of filtration system. I've heard of some companies working on things like that. No, it'd have to be smaller. Perhaps a new type of nanobot? And that data on the drive is needed to program it and test it in some off-world facility without a water cycle and atmosphere before releasing it on Earth . . ."

He's good. He doesn't even show an ounce of reaction.

But I *know* I'm right.

Rian rolls back his shoulders and stands. "Like I said, the work we're doing here is important. For a lot of people."

"But you're not going to tell me what it is."

Rian smiles; he knows I've guessed correctly. "I can't. It's a government secret."

"And that's why it's doomed," I snap back, the edge in my voice so sharp that even I'm surprised by it.

He stops, his expression slipping back into that placid mask. "Doomed?"

"You're government. The *Halifax* isn't, I guess you commandeered it, but you're in the government. That's why you're in charge of the mission, not the captain. And if this whole operation is *governmental* . . ."

"I didn't take you for an anarchist," Rian says dryly.

"I'm not. I mean, the government's *fine*, I don't care, it's just that . . . if you think the government can handle something as major as finding a solution to the environmental disaster that is Earth, you're deluded." I can't help but laugh, even when his face darkens.

But surely, he has to acknowledge that the United Galactic System is too big to do anything worthwhile. Small-scale, a society needs rules to function. But the further from the community, the more tangled the lines of authority get. The more chances for corruption or, worse, apathy. It's how Earth lost control of sovereign nations to global tourism boards. Used to be, laws came from one city that affected a whole country, then laws came from one planet that affected all the countries, and now things are coming from whole different worlds that affect all the rest. And the end result is a fucking mess by the time it trickles down. One government to oversee four worlds, each law passed down to increasingly distant micromanaging levels of rule before it goes into effect? Doesn't take rocket science to figure that's a game where only the law-makers get to win.

"It's an expensive program," he says. "And there are plenty of commercial outlets who would like to privatize the process and force the inhabitants of Earth to pay for clean air and water, but—"

"But the government is going to graciously step in and altruistically solve all the problems?"

"The system works," Rian protests. "It can be slow sometimes, unwieldy, but it works."

"For some people," I counter. "Eventually."

I like this, this fight. Because I can tell—he's a real believer. He's not so dumb as to think that any government is perfect, but he truly does think that by ticking the right boxes and going through the right protocols, he's going to make a difference.

He thinks he can play by the rules and still win.

I suppose that's been true for him all his life. But the rules were made for people like him.

Me? I know better than to believe in anyone else coming down to help, governmental or not. In the end, the only one fighting for your life is yourself, and trusting anyone to help without an angle of their own is what gets you killed. *Nothing* comes without cost. Every rescue mission comes with a bill.

Even this one.

"I fought to keep this project public," Rian says, his voice soft. "There were private investors who wanted to bankrupt the people of Earth for a chance at livable climate. You have no idea the work *so many* people have done to keep this project available to directly benefit the citizens instead of line the pockets of rich businesses. Which is why it is so important to make sure the drive and the cryptex

key, when we find it, don't end up in the hands of the highest bidder."

And suddenly, I don't want to fight anymore.

How can he not see that the highest bidder is always the
government that bids with power instead of coin?

16

The next morning, Rian finds me sitting in front of the airlock I first used to come aboard the *Halifax*.

"I'm surprised," he says, looking down at me. "I thought you'd be in the mess hall."

In answer, I raise the cup of porridge I already finished. The stuff had been thick with protein powder and vitamin supplements. It's liquid enough to suck up through a straw but chunky enough to need to be chewed, which is, frankly, the worst combination of edible textures that exists.

"Ah," he says, and then, to my surprise, he sits down beside me. "Shuttle launch in about an hour."

I nod, still looking up at the porthole window. I've got to suit up soon.

From this angle, I can't really see much of anything through the carbonglass. It's just a place to point my eyes at that's not him.

"You don't have to go," he says.

I bite the tip of my tongue. Not enough to draw blood. Just enough to focus on the pain instead of the possibility.

"This mission was designed to be run by Saraswati and Magnusson. You're a refugee; you don't have to—"

I finally turn to him, my lips curved into a smile. "Yeah, but if I find that key, we get to have steak and ice cream. And I'm much better than either of them, as proven already."

He grins at me, but his eyes—sharp as razorblades. The smile fades.

"That was brave of you, yesterday," he says. All sincerity. Like he needs me to believe it as much as he does.

"Saraswati said it was stupid."

"Saraswati thinks it was brave, too."

I have to give him a truth. If I don't, he'll tell. He thinks the danger's caught up with me, the fear. The enormity of the mission. That's not it. But I can't tell him why I'm in front of the airlock, why I'm not ready to jump onto the shuttle and head back to the planet. So, I have to give him something to hold on to, something that's as real as biting into a fresh peach.

"There's no such thing as bravery," I state clearly, looking right into his eyes.

His brow furrows. "What? No, bravery *is* real, and what you did, what you're doing—"

I shake my head. "I mean it. There is no such thing as bravery. Or cowardice, for that matter."

"Then what—"

"There is only survival."

He's waiting now. No more questions, no more back-and-forth. So I continue. "By definition, for an action to be brave, it has to be a choice, right? You have to see two options, at least, and you have to do the difficult one, the one that scares you, the one you know is right but wish wasn't. That's what bravery is."

"That's what you did," Rian says gently.

"No, you don't understand. The choice is fake. It's not real. Every action we take, *every* action we take, ultimately, we *never* choose to be brave or not. We just choose to survive."

I've turned, facing him entirely, and he's shifted too. This ship is big, but he's the only thing I see right now.

"It wasn't brave to climb up that rift yesterday," I say. "The alternative was . . ." I shrug. ". . . to die. Putting one foot in front of the other, climbing up one handhold at a time . . . that's just not bravery. It's survival. And that is true of everything."

I look down, not because I'm afraid of showing a lie but because it's harder to look someone in the face when you're telling the truth.

"Calling survival bravery . . . that fucks a person up. If someone gets sick, real sick? Months in the hospital, surgeries, experimental drugs . . . everyone calls that courage."

"Is it not?" Rian asks. His voice is all gentle; even his

eyes are soft. And that's when I know that telling him the worst truth inside me worked and kept him from seeing the worst lie. And I feel horrible for that, even in my triumph.

I shake my head. "Bravery's a choice, right? No one chooses to get sick like that. So, they're not brave. They're just surviving."

Because, I don't say, *you have to look at it the other way. If they're brave for living, you're saying they're a coward for dying.*

And that's not fair. They didn't choose that, either.

"I read your report," Rian says.

But that's not what he's really saying.

He's saying he got my background check. Last night, he wanted to celebrate. He didn't tell me everything he read. But he knows, and he can't keep it inside.

Pity always finds a way to leak out. It's like mold, hidden roots spreading rot inside that eventually has to burst out.

He read about what happened. The climate sickness. The way my father died.

And he's also saying he read about what came after.

Time to change the subject. Shift it to the right, so he doesn't see what's left.

I look up, grinning. "Petty theft, a spot of vandalism."

Rian quirks up an eyebrow. "Is that what you call anarchist messages hacked into the advertising system that went out to the whole European continent on Sol-Earth?" He used that word on purpose, *anarchist.* I'm not an anarchist.

I'm a realist. He just thinks that because last night I didn't hail him as a hero for working on Earth's environment, that I think the only other option to his government is no government.

I don't hate the government. I just don't think it's effective. He's never had a reason to doubt the system.

I've never had a reason to trust it.

"I just rearranged a few pixels in the ad sys." On millions of screens. "No lasting damage."

Besides, he and I both know I paid for that little crime, a fee that sent me to debt that sent me to space to scavenge ships and pay it off so I could avoid anything harsher.

You pay for everything in time or money. That's what Papa always said. But sometimes, a person doesn't have either. And that's why I learned to steal.

Rian huffs, and I can tell that he's a little amused by what I've said, how I've dismissed my crimes. Probably thinks I was just acting out, blowing off steam in my late teens. Now that I'm older, rebellion's been tempered out of me. Hard work has burned politics out of me, surely, and while I didn't throw a parade for this mission, I'm still willing to work it with him.

Why does everyone assume everything listed in a report is all there is? It's easy to get pegged for the little crimes. You only ever get pegged for the big ones once, and by then, the report's useless.

"So," I say, clapping my hands on my thighs before I get up. "You know my past. Don't worry. I've learned my lessons, and I'll get back to a scavenging rig and out of your hair soon enough, give you plenty of room to save the world."

Rian stands too. It's almost time to go. We've got to suit up, and that's not a task that can be rushed. But he doesn't start down the corridor. He's searching my face, and his eyes are sharp enough to cut my mask right off.

"The offer still stands," he says softly. "You can stay on the *Halifax* as long as you want. And eat all the lentils you can stomach."

I take a step closer to him. Too close. "But you're not going to be here, are you?" I say, voice as quiet as his. "You're not a crew member. You're going to get that key for the cryptex and leave."

"Maybe I like the idea of knowing where you'll be." A wry smile. "Just in case I need someone to dive headfirst toward a river of lava with a jetpack strapped to her back."

"I do leave a lasting impression, don't I?"

He opens his mouth to say something, but I never hear what it is, because I cross the last few centimeters between us and press my lips to his. I swallow his little gasp of surprise, but then his arms go around me, one hand on my back, pulling me tighter, one hand in my hair as he returns the kiss I gave him threefold.

I never know what I'm going to do until I do it, and I never know whether it's right or wrong until it's done, but this? This is right; this is right in a way my body knows before my mind does. And sure, maybe part of this is me filling up the adrenaline that emptied out yesterday, the hard knock of my heart reminding me that I'm still alive, I'm still in this game.

But there's something else here. Something I didn't expect.

Rian's all urgency, all suddenness, all hard strength that doesn't let go.

And me? I'm . . . letting him. His arms aren't just solid and strong and holding me against him. He's holding me up. My body's gone slack and willing and boneless.

If he lets me go, I wouldn't be able to stand on my own.

With one kiss, he's taken the gravity right out from under me.

But somehow, I'm not falling.

17

I't's past time to go.

I'm the last one to the shuttle bay.

My suit's on and checked and charged. Helmet under my arm. The door opens, and there's the crew, everyone but First. They're on guard duty, I assume. I get all the way down to the main floor. Magnusson's up the ramp into the shuttle, Saraswati a few steps behind him. Rian holds his arm out, offering to let me board first. And his eyes—

Those are going to haunt me.

"Wait," I say, and my smile's not easy but I know it looks like it is. "I forgot something."

Everyone looks at my suit—fully secure, already checked. My grin turns sheepish.

"We're going to be forever on that planet," I say. "I wanted . . ." I look from Rian to Nandina. It's easier to lie to her. "I need to get my data recorder. I was going to . . ."

I let the silence finish the fib. Nandina gets it immediately, I can tell. With a data recorder, I can switch to a private communication channel and record my thoughts. Give myself a little therapy and processing time while I scour the debris field in the wreckage.

"You have a data recorder?" Rian asks. Sharp, sharp.

"Be right back!" I say, spinning around and bounding toward the main corridor.

"You don't need—" Magnusson starts, but Nandina says to let me go.

There's a carbonglass window in the door, and I know through it, they can see me turn left in the direction of the bunk rooms. But I double back, bending over so they don't see me if they happen to still be looking. Once clear of the window, I run—I have to go fast. If they stop me now, it's all over. Starboard, then forward. Past the storage, round the bend. I've practiced this route; I spent the morning chewing on my porridge and counting the doors, the steps.

To the airlock.

As soon as I open the airlock door, an alarm's going to beep on the bridge. I figure I'll have *maybe* ten minutes then. I put my helmet on.

I open the door.

Step inside.

Slam it shut.

Seal the hatch.

There's a red light blinking over the door. The alarm's going.

I initiate the escape hatch depressurization. The screen

by the door starts counting down. The depressurization starts, and I know.

It's too late to go back now.

There's no override for an emergency protocol, especially not on a government-regulated ship. There's no way to open the inner door and go back inside. There's no way to stop the outer door from opening into black space. There's no way to keep me from stepping out into the nothing. One minute and fifty-four seconds, and it'll all be over.

I'll be gone.

Outside, through the porthole, Rian's face appears. Eyes wide, mouth open, shouting, but I can't hear anything through all the steel and carbonglass between us.

A new light flashes, a green one. The ship's open communication system. I tune my suit's comm link to the channel.

"Ada!" Rian roars, clenched fist on the porthole window.

"Sorry," I say.

"What are you doing?" he says. "Why are you here? Why—"

Then his face goes slack with horror. He turns away from the comm sys in the wall, shouts something.

He thinks I've stolen the cryptex drive.

But I haven't, and whatever response he gets from down the corridor confirms that. He whips back around to the porthole, staring through it like he wishes he could melt the carbonglass, reach through, and pull me back into the ship. Into his arms.

My stomach swoops. The gravity generator is shifting here in the airlock, prepping me for open space. According to the countdown, the depressurization is right on time. Forty-two seconds before the door opens and I step into the black of space.

"Sorry," I say again. I almost mean it. Just not for the reasons he thinks.

"For what?" Rian's voice is desperate. No one else is here. The others are probably at the shuttle still. It's not even been a full ten minutes since I walked away. The captain probably raced to the bridge when Rian realized I had been telling them goodbye with my delaying tactic.

I never had to go to my room to get my data recorder. It has not left my suit's outer pocket since I put it there just after Nandina gave it to me.

I've not answered Rian, but I know he's ticking through the possibilities. I doubt Nandina told him I got a data recorder, and even if she did, my excuse of wanting to talk through my problems to myself was a decent one. He didn't know the recorder was in my pocket the whole time yesterday.

The same pocket that held the cryptex drive.

I lean closer to the porthole window, watching his face

as the truth settles on him. The gravity's so low now that I'm floating. The air in this room is already gone; all my oxygen comes from my suit. Twenty-one seconds left. My helmet bumps against the window, and his eyes meet mine.

There's nothing left to say, no time to say it.

His fist unclenches, the flat of his palm on the glass.

I had the data recorder in my pocket when I put the cryptex drive I rescued inside. My jetpack was never broken. As if something like lava would mess with jaxon jets. I've *been* telling them that my pack is good quality. It's not my fault no one listened. I put the jetpack on standby and forced myself to do the excruciatingly slow climb up to give the drive time to copy its contents onto the data recorder. Everything I did while climbing up the rift was a delay tactic.

I never had to steal the cryptex drive. I just had to steal the information on it.

"But you don't have the key," he says.

The outer door opens. Behind me, there's the wreckage of my ship, *Glory*, the hull breached. And there's all of space and eternity, countless stars surrounded by the killing void.

In front of me is Rian.

"You're asking the wrong question," I say.

"Then what should I be asking?" His voice is raw, desperate.

And I think, *He's thinks he's supposed to ask me to stay.*

I sigh. He's going to be so mad at himself for not figuring this out sooner.

I put my gloved hand over the window, my fingers lining up with his splayed hand on the other side of the glass.

"You need to ask why there were no bodies in the wreck," I say. "Check with Magnusson. He saw the empty bridge. No harnesses strapped. No bodies. And when you go down and look at the cargo section . . . no bodies. None."

And then I push away, floating out of the *Halifax* and into the black.

18

I turn my back to the *Halifax*.

I ignite my jetpack, soaring straight to *Glory*'s airlock door, still open from when I left my ship, desperate and dying.

That part was real. My air tank was almost empty by the time they bothered to pick me up.

But I could have recharged it if I had to.

What can I say? I love a dramatic entrance.

The breach in my ship is real. But the explosion—the one *I set*—did not compromise the electricals or the life support. I made sure of that. I couldn't risk something as nebulous as a random mayday; I needed a real distress call, a real problem. I may have exaggerated it a tiny bit, but I was counting on no one looking too closely. Rian sent out drones to inspect the damage. Had he suited up and looked for himself, he might have seen more than I wanted him to.

As soon as I go through the hole by my own ship's airlock, I use the grab bars to pull myself into the main body. The power's offline, which means the gravity generator's not on. I'm still floating, going from point to point through my ship.

When I get closer to my cockpit, I go through the bulkhead doors, then turn around and seal them.

The back half of my ship is still breached. Can't properly fix that hole now. But the bulkhead door seals the front half entirely. The massive steel door bisects my ship, and it's easy enough to just close the door, lock it, and boot up the power and start the process of repressurizing and re-oxygenating *this* part of the ship. It doesn't take long. Soon enough, my boots hit the floor. By the time I'm strapped into my pilot seat, *Glory*'s ready to fly again.

This is the dangerous bit, I think. *Leaving.*

I pull off my helmet and take a deep breath of the oxygen that had been stored in the tanks, waiting for me to come back home.

There's a communication signal hailing me. *Halifax* is reaching out.

Rian wants to talk.

What else is there to say?

He already knows that I stole the data off the cryptex drive. And soon enough, he's going to figure it out on his own that the reason why I could leave now is because I *already* have the key.

I check it, just to be sure. And it's right there, locked in the bridge box. That is a safe place to store something.

I get my engine running. *Halifax* might try to chase me, sure, but it's been running cold, letting the shuttle do the work. And my *Glory* is small and nimble. And I've already got an encrypted portal code locked and ready.

I veer out of orbit around the planet, away from the salvage site. I was here before the crash even happened, as arranged. I watched as the crew evacuated on their escape shuttle, made sure they met with their contact and got out of the system after they set the ship to crash-land onto the planet. It hadn't been a great choice of crash, but it was the most viable planet along the route. Considering most of the universe is black void, having a land-based planet on the route at all was a lucky break.

The cryptex key was always going to be the hard thing to find. It's tiny, innocuous, and uncrackable. The crew had told me before about where they suspected it was going to be hidden, but they hadn't been sure. That was the problem with something this high-security. This valuable. The crew hadn't been consulted on where everything was hidden. They hadn't even been told of *what* they were carrying.

But I knew. And when I told them, and when I paid them—using my client's money, of course—the crew let me convince them to take an *alternative* route home.

It took me three days to track the key down, longer than I'd anticipated.

Long enough for the *Halifax* to show up before I'd gotten

my hands on the cryptex drive. At least I'd been on the ship when I got the warning that they were in range. It gave me time to breach my own ship's hull, put on a suit, and wait to be saved.

I glance at the blinking light that signals the *Halifax* trying to open communication with me.

I turn off the comms.

"One goal," I whisper, blinking rapidly.

My hands settle over the controls of *Glory*.

"Full speed." My voice is stronger this time.

I soar away through the stars.

DEPARTMENT OF
INTERGALACTIC BIOTECHNOLOGY

CLASSIFIED INFORMATION

Report compiled by:

Rian C. White, Covert Field Operative

Distress signal from *Roundabout* was sent out at 13.98.324.

Launch of *Halifax* by 14.15.641. Commandeered government-funded research vessel for rescue of any surviving crew[1] and salvage of the plans and prototype developed by [CENSORED] for the benefit of Sol-Earth's climate.

Arrived in sector at 18.24.136. Immediately received a distress signal from a D-class salvage rig with local identifier *Glory,* Sol-Earth registry: #5O213-JLN.

As mission operative, I ordered Captain Ursula Io to delay response to *Glory* until further information could be determined. Primary upload took a quarter-cycle to receive and revealed the registry owner of *Glory* was Ada Jane Lamarr of New Valetta, Malta, Sol-Earth. Despite some initial crimes listed in the report,[2] I deemed Lamarr to not be a threat. Ref-

---

1 Ada was right. Further inspection of the wreckage revealed *no* human remains. Escape pods had been deployed, but there is no evidence of them anywhere, and the transponder attached to the escape pods was removed. Sabotage from crew?

2 I've gone over the reports a million times. There was zero indication that Ada was working with a larger-scale rebellion, but there's also no way she could have done this heist by herself. She had outside help. Who? Of note: she didn't pick up on the identifying code for the most well-known group . . .

uge accepted, Lamarr boarded *Halifax* and received initial medical treatment from the med officer on duty.

Lamarr reported to have already been on the ground, salvaging scrap metal, confirmed via drone, which revealed a stowage of scraps in her cargo haul. Her reports supported our initial scans of the surface of the planet, namely:

- *Roundabout* impacted with the planet surface and broke in two main pieces.[3]

- The forward of the ship was in the more precarious position.

- The aft was at least one klick away from the forward, with an extensive field of debris.

MISSION: Secure encrypted data on drive as well as the accompanying cryptex key and nanobot prototype.[4]

STATUS: Failure

REPORT: After receiving advice from ground crew Saraswati Yadav and Baldur Magnusson, I determined that the drive had been stored in the bridge box and had been projected through the carbonglass viewport on impact. Magnusson located the safe box it was in, and it looked likely to be unharmed, despite its precarious position on a ridge. Yadav

---

3 She told me, didn't she? The ship didn't crash right. It was crashed *intentionally*.

4 That's the thing I never told her about. But she got it anyway. Without the prototype, the entire mission is in jeopardy. The data can be retrieved via a new upload from the source. But the prototype . . . Perhaps [CENSORED] can remake it?

and Magnusson initially attempted to retrieve the safe box via a magna-lock hook, drone crane, and mechanical lift.

Seismic activity on the planet surface impeded progress. The safe box shifted onto a lower ledge. Other attempts to retrieve the drive failed.

Lamarr presented a unique solution. Her LifePack was equipped with a jaxon jet[5] that was fully operational, and her thincraft suit[6] could withstand the heat of the exposed lava river at the base of the cliff long enough to retrieve the safe box.

The following day, Lamarr retrieved the drive at great personal risk.[7][8]

The next morning, however, it was discovered that Lamarr had made an illegal copy of the data on the drive using a personal recording device I had been unaware of. The data recorder had been given to her by a member of crew who did not suspect Lamarr's intent. Suggest no punishment to the crew member.

Since Lamarr exited *Halifax* and returned to her personal ship with the data, I have commanded a thorough examination of the remaining debris field. No trace of the cryptex key

---

5 I noted her jetpack early on. A nice unit. Worth more than her scrap pile of a ship. That should have been a clue. Why did I not piece this shit together? She told me everything. I just didn't listen.

6 Of course I scanned her suit records. She was a scavenger and had logged a few legit jobs. I should have seen the blank spots she erased. I kept the data, obviously, but I can't seem to find any connection to the locator information and . . . anything. Yet. She was thorough, though. She purposefully created logs of her hauling scrap metal to match the cargo in her hold and her own cover story.

7 Was it, though? I inspected that jaxon jet myself. It made sense at the time the heat would have compromised it . . . but no. No. *She* put her jetpack on standby, didn't she? She made herself climb out of that ridge instead of using it so she had time to copy all the data onto the drive . . . Why didn't I see that before?

8 I know why I didn't see it before. Because she didn't want me to. All that talk about . . .

or the nanobot prototype that was stored with it has been found. I have located the UGS *Roundabout*'s recorder box; report attached.[9]

A possible conclusion that must be considered is that Lamarr had previously found the key and prototype prior to making contact with the ship, which would mean the data is compromised.

CONCLUSION: Without the key, the information on the cryptex drive is not accessible. The source may be able to provide a replica at great expense, but the more pressing concern is that Lamarr can sell[10] the current data.[11] [12] [13] [14]

---

9 It's been corrupted, though. From the location and state we found it in, I think this wasn't done by Ada. She had help.

10 What the fuck is she going to do with the drive? Sell it? Does she even know what is on it and how important it is and how many lives are at stake???

11 Does she even care?

12 She does. I know she does. She couldn't have faked it all. Could she have?

13 WHO IS SHE WORKING WITH? And why?

14 *Fuck, fuck, fuck, fuck. FUCK.*

01010100 01101000 01101001 01110011 00100000
01100100 01100001 01110100 01100001 00100000
01101000 01100001 01110011 00100000 01100010
01100101 01100101 01101110 00100000 01100011
01101111 01101101 01110000 01110010 01101111
01101101 01101001 01110011 01100101 01100100
00101110 00100000 01010100 01101000 01101001
01110011 00100000 01100100 01100001 01110100
01100001 00100000 01101000 01100001 01110011
00100000 01100010 01100101 01100101 01101110
00100000 01100011 01101111 01101101 01110000
01110010 01101111 01101101 01101001 01110011
01100101 01100100 00101110 00100000 01010100
01101000 01101001 01110011 00100000 01100100
01100001 01110100 01100001 00100000 01101000
01100001 01110010 01101111 01101101 01101001
01110011 01100101 01100100 00101110 00100000
01010100 01101000 01101001 01110011 00100000
01100100 01100001 01110100 01100001 00100000
01101000 01100001 01110010 01101111 01101101
01101001 01110011 01100101 01100100 00101110
01101001 01110011 01100101 01100100 00101110
01101001 01110011 01100101 01100100 00101110
01101001 01110011 01100101 01100100 00101110 001

DEPARTMENT OF
INTERGALACTIC BIOTECHNOLOGY

CLASSIFIED INFORMATION

Report compiled by:

Rian C. White, Covert Field Operative

After extensive analysis of all available data, including field reports, drone footage, and simulations, it is the conclusion of our team, led by Dr. Harold Krumlov,[1] that the UGS *Roundabout* did not crash due to any ship malfunction.[2][3]

It is impossible to know how much was lost in the crash.[4]

It is unfortunate the ship crashed on a protoplanet with such a violent and unsteady natural environment.[5][6]

---

1 Good guy. I trust him.

2 I can't prove it, but it's my belief that the crew evacuated the ship and set it on a crash course to the planet. They probably tried to angle it in a way that wouldn't cause too much destruction, but they couldn't take into consideration the conditions of the planet. This accounts for (a) the lack of bodies and also (b) the lack of access to the drive and key. The crew, which must be working for Ada and/or whoever she's working for, enabled the ship to be looted in part because they could not access the drive and the key/prototype.

3 Harry confirmed: the drive had been locked in the bridge box that had a separate alarm system. The crew had no way of knowing whether or not removing the drive from the bridge box would have triggered an automatic erasure. And the key/prototype were hidden within cargo purposefully in an effort to prevent any corruption by the crew.

4 Also impossible to know how long Ada was there. If she orchestrated or at least knew of the crash in advance . . . she said she was on the site for only two days. That now seems *very* unlikely. She could have been there a week or more, located the key, and then started to figure out how to get the drive . . .

5 I've checked the routes. That planet was the *only* terran-based planet on the path. Short of crashing into a gas giant or a star, the only other option was to ghost the ship, which would have had other ramifications.

6 New theory: The operation that ran this con employed Ada to act as salvage but hoped that she would find the drive and key before *Halifax* or other backup arrived. When Ada got word of the *Halifax* being in range, she covered her tracks by sabotaging her own ship and infiltrating herself into *my* crew.

DEPARTMENT OF INTERGALACTIC INTELLIGENCE

RIAN WHITE: Hey, quick question.

JAMIE NIX: A quick question, already encrypted in a secure chat? This should be good.

RW: It's about the *Roundabout* fiasco.

JN: What a cock-up. Were you reprimanded? Hate to be on the bad side of—

RW: No. I'm clear. But yeah . . . it's a cock-up.

JN: What's the Q?

RW: That code phrase the Sol-Earth group uses—asking someone if they know Jane Irwin.

JN: Yeah?

RW: Can you confirm if that code is still used? Not compromised or anything.

JN: That's one of my top checks. I have active agents who still report it's good. Why?

RW: I used that code phrase on the saboteur. She showed no recognition.

JN: Maybe she's not with the Sol-Earth group.

JN: Or maybe she's got a really good poker face.

RW: . . . yeah.

JN: Have you seen the latest reports on that group? Want me to send them to you?

RW: Yes, please.

DEPARTMENT OF
INTERGALACTIC INTELLIGENCE

SUBJECT: [BLANK]
MARKED: TOP SECRET
ATTACHMENT: CN GREEN ROGUE REPORT
Highest level of encryption

From: Jamie Nix, Doll
To: Rian C. White, DolBiTe

Hey Rian,

Here's the report. After our chat, I triple-checked. "Jane Irwin" is still a commonly used code phrase among the group. Either your mark didn't react, or she's not in the group, maybe doesn't even know about the group.[1] It's used for recruitment and confirmation of contacts. It's a low-level phrase, in other words, and can be enhanced with specific follow-ups to the phrase for viability.

We have yet to identify the top members of this organization, or even to know what they call themselves. As you know, we use the code name *Green Rogue* when referring to what we think is their activity. They have marked different methods from other, more extremist groups.[2]

---

1 No, that doesn't seem likely. Ada would know. She would know. I'm certain of it. She's just a better liar than I thought before.

2 God, I hope Ada's working for something like this group rather than the Jarra.

Anyway, none of this is new information. You can read the full report, but the basics are all the same:

1. Green Rogue believes the intergalactic government is too large and unlikely to provide any real aid, but they are not willing to lead their members toward secession . . . yet. Agents disagree on whether or not this is the ultimate goal. Members consider themselves in a Robin Hood–like role—steal from the rich, give to the people of Earth. There are separate branches, some focused on acquiring and others focused on redistribution. The network is vast and, because it supports the people, is well-hidden. **It's unlikely that locals will undermine the operations at play here.**[3]

2. No overarching focus has yet been declared publicly by Green Rogue. This is a group that *has* motives, but the higher-up members are not transparent.[4] (Note: this works toward recruitment. They state goals that benefit Sol-Earth, bring new members into the fold, and then, once people move up the ranks, the motives become more opaque and secretive.)

   There have been some legitimately good things the group's done, if not exactly legal things. All of this leads me to question if this is part of a *far larger* plan that we've previously been

---

3 Unlikely but not impossible. That about sums up Ada, anyway.

4 "Not transparent" also sums up Ada. Could she be leading this group? She's young for it, but she could have moved up the ranks . . . Her record stops after that one teenaged prank with the ad system. I'd thought maybe she'd cleaned up her act after that, but what if her records were expunged by this group in order to clear her for new work? (Note to self: Lamarr. Not Ada. Lamarr.)

unaware of, or if your situation[5] isn't really operating under the cover of Green Rogue. I'll have select agents put some feelers out for information on the cryptex and nanobot.

POSTSCRIPT: Okay, but here's the thing, Rian. Can I be honest? On the one hand, Green Rogue has serious issues with [CENSORED], so I could see them undermining your efforts, since it's linked to him. But they wouldn't really block such a good development[6] for Sol-Earth. That's not really in their MO. I can see why you're linking your situation[7] to this group, but . . . there's a missing piece.[8]

---

5 Nice way of saying it. *Cock-up* was more accurate.

6 That's the thing. The nanobots really will save billions of people's lives. They could save all of Sol-Earth. Jamie's right—I'm missing something. But *that* is linked to it. At the end of the day, I just don't think ~~Ada Lamarr~~ *Ada* would ~~actively do something that would hurt Sol-Earth. Even if there were chicken cutlets and mashed potatoes on the table.~~

7 Cock-up

8 Understatement of the year.

DEPARTMENT OF
INTERGALACTIC HISTORY

SUBJECT: DATA REQUEST, *ROSE*

From: Sara Graham, Record Locator
To: Rian C. White, DolBiTe

Dear Mr. White,

As you requested, I have obtained the available information on a lost ship with the local identifier of *Rose*. I have found a ship matching that description (Registry #6J876-LMX), reported as lost about two and a half years ago.[1] I will send the full report through momentarily but wanted to personally confirm the details in question: The crew comprised of eight members of the Shah family, all of whom perished due to an oxygen vent that may have resulted from a minor ship malfunction.

Sincerely,
Sara

---

1 If nothing else, this was true.

DEPARTMENT OF
INTERGALACTIC TRANSPORT

SUBJECT: CREW LOG, UGS ROUNDABOUT
FROM: MANDARIA ORGU, SCHEDULER
TO: RIAN C. WHITE, DOITE

Mr. White:

After extensive internal investigation, I can confirm that all logs of the crew for the UGS *Roundabout*'s last mission have been scrubbed.[1] Multiple schedule shifts and logs amongst all viable crew members[2] have obscured records,[3] and we seem to have a data breach.[4] My supervisor will be meeting with you soon.[5]

—MO

---

1 This is the part that shocks me. The crew was in on it. I've looked over every single possible manifest. Everyone employed with access to the *Roundabout* is somehow on other rosters. There's not only no record of who was on the crew, there are no employees unaccounted for.

2 Of note: Every. Single. Member. Of the potential crew roster is from Sol-Earth. Is that connected? Possible. They're at minimum all covering for each other, but some of them had to be actively involved.

3 Fuck, this is so much bigger than one woman. This is a wide-scale operation. Who's behind it? Who's the mastermind? ~~What is Ada's role in this? How can we retrieve the tech?~~

4 She *has* to be working for someone. Someone rich enough to fund a heist of this magnitude. Private commercial enterprises? Anarchist group? Rebellion?

5 This should be fun. How could a crew just disappear? Someone's going to lose a job over this. And we have to find a way to update security servers.

MEMO: Upcoming Charity Fundraiser Security

All staff, be advised. The upcoming charitable fundraiser will feature multiple high-value assets[1] that will require all hands on deck to insure the safety of both the items and the guests, especially host Strom Fetor.[2] Additional security training is mandatory for all operatives.[3] [4]

---

1 If she's willing to sell data like the cryptex drive to the highest bidder, she'll be willing to steal something here . . .

2 Ada noted that there was Fetor Tech in the cargo hold of the *Roundabout*. Before, I assumed she didn't know of the link between Fetor and the nanobots, but now . . .

3 If she targets this event, I need to be ready. I can't let her escape again.

4 She's mine.

ACKNOWLEDGMENTS

This book would not exist if I hadn't gotten really, *really* pissed off one hot night while in Phoenix, Arizona. I was at a convention—shoutout to Phoenix Fan Fusion!—and while everyone was generally very lovely and wonderful, one person gave me such a backhanded compliment that I wrote this entire book in a fit of rage just to prove that person wrong. (Don't worry; he doesn't know this song is about him.) Rather than sleep after a long day of book signings and panels, fueled by spite and rage, I cancelled drinks with friends and sat in my hotel room and started choking the oxygen out of Ada.

A good time was had by all.

Ada Lamarr is named after two of my favorite women in science: Ada Lovelace and Hedy Lamarr. Both of these women are hotter than you and smarter than you, but they're both too polite and too dead to tell you that (I'm neither).

My thanks to Merrilee Heifetz, my brilliant agent, and her assistant Rebecca Eskildsen for getting this book in front of Ben Schrank, the publisher who launched my career with *Across the Universe* and who put this book into the hands of Navah Wolfe, who I've wanted to work with for ages. In many ways, this book is a culmination and a coming home. I wrote *Across the Universe* in a fit of desperation, my last attempt after a decade of trying to break into a career as an author. I wrote *Full Speed* under different circumstances, but there's true joy in working with some of the same people who made my first dreams come true, and who continue to be foundational in helping me and so many others tell the stories of our hearts, whether they're pure or filled with spite.

Reader, you may have spotted a few *Across the Universe* links and allusions. Whether you've been with me since day one or you found me through Ada, I truly appreciate your magic in bringing ink to life in your imagination. Thank you, sincerely.

Everyone at the DAW team has been a dream, and I am truly so honored to get to work with them all. I do not remember a time when I didn't have DAW books on my shelf. Navah, I'm still pinching myself at how lucky Ada and I are to find such a champion in you! Madeline Goldberg, thank you for all you do to keep us organized and on track. Sarah Christensen Fu, thank you for coordinating publicity and marketing and making sure the world knows about my chaos thief. My thanks also to managing editor Joshua Starr and production supervisor Elizabeth Koehler for all you do to keep brilliant stories in the hands of readers. And of course, my gratitude to Betsy Wollheim, DAW's publisher who oversees it all.

I also want to thank Jennifer Randolph, my childhood bestie who grew up to work in an actually useful job as a marine biologist. Her experience with SCUBA diving and her gracious answering of my prodding questions allowed me to write what I hope is a realistic experience of running out of air. If not, blame Ada.

Cheers to my Wordsmith friends, who spurred on my spitefulness and wrote words alongside me every week, especially Cristin, Lee, and Laura!

Sincerest apologies to my mother, who requested I take out the "fucks" in this book, who still fucking loves me even though I added more. Love to my son, who had no idea what this book was about and still provided me with lots of "helpful" advice on putting in more pitfall traps, and to my husband, who tried to offer helpful advice in between our son's attempts to pitch more explosions. I should also thank my dog. She didn't really help in any way, but she is cute, so there's that.